The Shiver in the Arctic

Greenland Missing Persons #3

featuring Constable Petra "Piitalaat" Jensen

Don't miss novella #4 in the
Greenland Missing Persons series
The Fever in the Water

Published by Aarluuk Press

ISBN: 978-87-93957-65-7

www.christoffer-petersen.com

Author's Note

The Shiver in the Arctic is the third novella in the Greenland Missing Persons series featuring Constable Petra Piitalaat Jensen. Readers of my other novellas will know that I like to experiment a little with each story, whereas the novels are more uniform in style. So, if this novella tastes a little like a *whodunnit*, then you're not wrong, your eyes are not deceiving you, although I sincerely hope you will be deceived at some point in the story.

The Shiver in the Arctic is packed with cultural Easter eggs, bringing a little slice of Greenland into your life. It is also longer than my usual novellas and for that I blame Petra.

Chris
July 2020
Denmark

The Shiver in the Arctic

Greenland Missing Persons #3

Part 1

It was the magazine article that did it. From the moment Sergeant Kiiu "George" Duneq discovered that a freelance journalist was writing a piece about the Greenland Missing Persons desk, he did his very best to thwart it, even sending me on two weeks of prisoner escort duty, to get me out of the capital. Of course, he hadn't realised that the journalist was writing the article for *Suluk*, Air Greenland's in-flight magazine, and we met at the airport at the start of my prisoner escort duties.

"Actually, it was your commissioner who let me know where you'd be," the journalist told me over coffee in Nuuk's tiny Arctic airport.

"Really?"

"Yes," he said, with a theatrical turning of the pages of his spiral-bound notebook. "He speaks very highly of you."

I thought of Atii Napa, my long-suffering girlfriend from the academy, the second my cheeks started to flush. She would have teased me about it, together with a comment or two about the young journalist's looks. Of course, if she had been there, during the interview, she might even have given me a few pointers as to how to respond. Atii often acted as my mirror during those moments when a man flirted with me, teasing me at how obvious it was, and questioning just how I could be so oblivious of it. She was usually right. While I might blush at a few complements, I often needed the sledgehammer approach when it came to picking up on a man's underlying intentions.

And yet, at the crowded table in the airport waiting lounge, the journalist had enough trouble prying the story out of me, let alone asking me for dinner – if that was even his intention.

"I've been lucky," I said, as my cheeks cooled, and my usual skin colour paled to a light creamy brown, typical among many of my fellow Greenlanders, but not all, as European blood was a big part of many Greenlanders' DNA. "The commissioner is very supportive."

"Putting you – a newly graduated constable – in charge of the Greenland Missing Persons department."

"*Desk*," I said, correcting him. "A very small one."

I was tempted to let him write about the *department*, if only to enjoy the sight of Sergeant Duneq's generous jowls quivering with rage. The fact that I, a lowly constable fresh out of the academy, had a dusty desk with a broken chair irked him beyond all reason, but having a whole department... I let the thought linger, like a delicious morsel deliberately left on the side of one's plate, something I could enjoy later, when flying to yet another town to escort yet another prisoner from one jail to another.

"But you are responsible for investigating cases about missing persons in Greenland?"

"I answer the phone," I said.

"Oh, I think you do a little more than that, Constable."

I glanced at the passengers sitting beside us as the journalist checked his notes. With such a small population, Greenlanders shared a strange sense of polite intimacy. It didn't mean that we were entitled to know each other's business, but more often than not we did, if only because of the many threads and personal relations connecting the people across the country. Even so, it could be embarrassing at times, and I spared a mental thanks for whoever had issued me with an overly large police jacket with the stiff collar, behind which I could dip my head.

"You looked for a boy in Qaanaaq?" the journalist said.

"Yes."

"And, more recently, you were involved in a search for a girl in Kangaamiut."

"That's right."

"Two cases, both involving children. Is that typical of a missing persons case in Greenland?"

"I think it was coincidence," I said.

"The boy was missing for nearly a year, and the girl for about three days."

"Yes," I said, frowning as I tried to anticipate his follow-up question.

"And you needed help, in both cases."

"I coordinated with the local police each time."

"Right, but that's not what I meant," he said.

I knew it wasn't. I could see his notes, and there were too many of them scribbled beside the names of the people who had helped me, and far too many question marks for him to ignore them.

"Tell me about Tuukula," he said.

"He lives in Qaanaaq, with his daughter."

"Luui?"

"Yes," I said, smiling at the thought of Luui's tangle of wild black hair, and the freckles striped across her button nose. "She's five."

"And Tuukula helped you in Qaanaaq?"

"They both did."

"And again, in Kangaamiut. But that time…" The journalist paused to check his notes. "You asked for Tuukula's help." He looked up and smiled. "Is he a police consultant?"

"I don't speak Greenlandic," I said, wondering just how much I should reveal about Tuukula's role in my investigations. "He translates for me."

"So, he's a translator?"

"No," I said. "He's a shaman." The word slipped out, before I could stop myself.

"I see," the journalist said, but I could tell that he didn't. The bemused look he wore complemented the look on the faces of the passengers sitting beside us.

"It's complicated," I said, by way of an explanation. "Tuukula seems to be in the right place at the right time, and his daughter…"

"Yes?"

I bit my lip, wishing I hadn't brought Luui into it. It was difficult enough for *me* to appreciate her role in each investigation, and nigh on impossible for strangers to grasp. I settled on one truth, while ignoring the more challenging aspect of her uncanny ability to *see* things that the adults around her missed.

"Luui is quite the charmer," I said. "She disarms people. No," I said, shaking my head as the journalist added to his notes, "that's not the right word. I should have said she puts them at ease."

"And her father? Apart from translating, does he put people at ease too, or does he have other skills that help you solve missing persons cases?"

I had to pause for a moment, as I wondered how to frame my response. The couple next to me leaned in, ever so slightly, as if they were just as eager for the answer as the journalist. I could have embellished Tuukula's role of translation, but at the risk of making a joke of the Greenland Missing Persons desk, I didn't want to ignore his practical skills as a hunter, and the supernatural intuition of the shaman.

"Tuukula is…"

"Yes?"

It was harder than I imagined to put my finger on what he did or didn't do, that helped each case. If Luui had been there, she might have bunched her tiny hand into a small fist, before exploding her fingers with a *poof*, followed by the English word *magic*.

Magic.

There was plenty to be found in Greenland, but the rational and professional part of my mind kicked in, and I remembered the benevolence of Police Commissioner Lars Andersen and I owed it to him and my colleagues to maintain a positive image of the police in Greenland.

"Tuukula is my translator, and my guide in

areas unfamiliar to me."

"Like the spirit world?" the journalist asked, prying.

"Greenland," I said, as my flight was announced over the loudspeaker. "Thank you, but I have to go."

"Just a second," he said, as he pulled out his smartphone. "I need a photo for the article."

As soon as he had taken the photo, I pushed my chair back from the table, and then joined the queue of passengers waiting to board the De Havilland Dash 7 bound for Tasiilaq on Greenland's east coast. Sergeant Duneq planned for me to return that same day, before flying north to Ilulissat and then on to Uummannaq. The journalist promised that I would be able to read a shorter version of his article online by the end of the day.

"It's a teaser for the main piece," he said, as he caught up with me in the queue. "Just to get people interested. It'll be in all three languages, of course. Online and in print in Greenlandic, Danish and English."

"English?"

"You do speak English?" he asked.

"Yes," I said. "It's just Greenlandic that I struggle with."

"Which is why you need Tuukula?"

He was fishing for one last quote, that last piece of magic. But even though I could clearly see and hear Luui saying the word in my mind, I did little more than smile and nod farewell, before stuffing my hands into my jacket pockets and walking to the gate.

They had promised snow later in the week, but even a city girl like me could see that it was already on its way. I patted my pockets to check that I hadn't lost my essentials including my toothbrush, phone charger, a couple of Mars bars, and extra sanitary pads – things I would need if stranded away from home – and then walked the short distance to board the plane.

The commissioner might have spoiled Duneq's plans to stop the interview, but I was still stuck on a flight going east, with the very real threat of being stranded in an airport if the storm caught up with me. I slipped my earbuds into my ears as soon as I found my seat, tuning into my current playlist as the stewardess seated the remaining passengers.

"Magic," I said, as the slow beat of Coldplay's song filtered into my ears.

Part 2

The weather was better in Tunu, the Greenlandic name for the east coast of Greenland. I blinked in the sun as it reflected off the snow, chatting with the airport staff, while we waited for the helicopter from Tasiilaq, the largest town on the east coast. With a population of just over two thousand residents, it was nine times smaller than Nuuk, a fact that always made me smile. It was no secret amongst our friends and colleagues that Atii and I dreamed of living in a big city, and that we thought of Nuuk as the first step before somewhere bigger such as New York or London. Sure, Copenhagen was another option, but I had my sights set further afield.

The shudder of the rotor blades pressing against the airport windows tugged me out of conversation and back into work mode, as I prepared to receive my prisoner for the flight back to Nuuk. Even by Greenlandic standards, Tikaajaat was considered a petty criminal, an opportunist. But it seemed that, lately, he had exploited a long string of opportunities and the locals were tired of him. As Tasiilaq fell under the same municipality as Nuuk, I was tasked with bringing Tikaajaat to the capital, in part to relieve Tasiilaq of his problematic behaviour, but also to spare him from potential harm as his family, his neighbours, and even the people he used to call friends, turned against him. The black eye he wore, together with his limp, suggested that the time was right, that he had received a lesson, but that his teachers had yet to punish Tikaajaat further, as so often happened in the small Greenlandic communities.

"I'm not innocent," Tikaajaat said in Danish, as he buckled into the window seat of the return flight to Nuuk.

"You mean you're guilty?"

"*Iiji*," he said, with a vigorous nod of his small head. "Very."

I hid a smile as he started to list his sins, tapping his fingers for each crime of theft, including stealing alcohol, bullets, money, and cigarettes.

"And one pair of underpants," he said.

"Underpants?"

I'm not sure if I was supposed to talk to Tikaajaat while he was in my custody, but the flight was practically empty and, sitting at the very back of the aircraft, the drone of the Dash 7's four propellers prevented any of the other passengers from hearing what Tikaajaat had to say.

"Worn once," he said.

"The underpants?"

"*Iiji.*"

"And you took them?"

Tikaajaat shrugged. "It was cheaper and easier than cleaning my own."

"Right," I said, stifling another smile.

I took a moment to look at Tikaajaat, trying to see past his black eye, the tangle of black greasy hair plastered slick and sweaty on his forehead, his chipped and broken teeth. I wanted to see *him*, if only for a moment, to try to understand what might compel a young man to steal a pair of underpants. My dreams of New York were interrupted by the thought that life in Nuuk – rather, *my* life in Nuuk, was easier in so many ways than Tikaajaat's life in Tasiilaq. I had a regular income – and a good one, by many standards. I had a modern flat, and friends to pick me up when I was down. And yet, it was still possible to see something of myself in Tikaajaat's deep brown eyes, to remember that as a young girl, I had also stolen things – small things, the kind that made a big difference. As a teenager, I had often railed against the rules of the Children's Home, but maybe those rules, and a roof over my head, had been the difference between who Tikaajaat was and who I had become.

"How old are you?" I asked.

"Twenty-three."

We were the same age.

Tikaajaat chatted all the way from Kulusuk to Nuuk, slurping two cups of creamy coffee, and one can of coke. I gave him my cellophane-wrapped biscuit, curious at the care with which he opened it, pressing a wet fingertip to collect the crumbs from the corners of the wrapper. I remembered the bar of chocolate in the cargo pocket on my uniform trousers and pressed it into Tikaajaat's hands. The look he gave me, before he opened it, was just a little too much for me, and I turned away, calling the stewardess to ask for more coffee, in an attempt to hide a sudden swirl of pity surging through my body.

While Sergeant Duneq – *Jowls*, as I called him – might be the bane of my police life, I couldn't help but wonder if, in his own way, he was just trying to toughen me up, and escorting Tikaajaat back to Nuuk was just one more opportunity for me to learn even more about my people.

Tikaajaat slept beside me, his head pressed on my shoulder, and I said nothing more until we landed, rousing him gently before the wheels thudded into the runway.

"Good luck," I said to Tikaajaat, as I handed him over to my colleagues waiting with the patrol car outside the airport.

"You're not coming back to the station?" said Constable Kuno Schmidt, raising his voice over the wind. The Danish police officer blinked in the light snow flurrying across the car park.

"No," I said. "I have to fly north for the next one. Duneq's orders."

"North?" Schmidt pointed at the grey snow clouds pressing in from the sea. "You'll get stranded up there, if you even get that far."

"I think that's part of Duneq's plan." I tried to smile, but the wind caught my hair. I clawed it from my face, waved at Tikaajaat in the back seat, and then jogged back to the airport building. The wind was coming from the south – a strong tailwind to push us north. *We'll make good time,* I thought. *If we leave now.* The flight was boarding, and I joined the queue of passengers, their heads swivelling as they swapped glances with each other, nodding at the weather, then shuffling forward, eager to ride ahead of the storm.

Part 3

The flight should have taken the coastal route, making a sharp right-angled landing at Maniitsoq, then flying on to Aasiaat after a short break, before landing at the slightly larger airport of Ilulissat, the gateway to the north. But the wind cupping the tail of the Dash 7 encouraged the pilots to keep going, ignoring the protests of the passengers headed for the two smaller towns on the route, as they adjusted course for Ilulissat. I didn't mind, for two reasons. I was scheduled to fly on from Ilulissat to Qaarsut and then Uummannaq, by helicopter. But if I was going to be stranded – a common occurrence in Greenland – then I'd choose Ilulissat every time. The hotels were bigger and better, and Air Greenland would be footing the bill. With the exorbitant rents in Nuuk, being stranded in a luxury hotel in Ilulissat was almost like a vacation, one that I could afford.

We flew out of the clutches of the storm, leaving the turbulence behind us, and landing in Ilulissat ahead of schedule. Passengers flying further north were encouraged to leave the aircraft first, in order to catch their connecting flights, quashing any secret hopes I might have had about a forced stay in a hotel, as the ground crew hurried us from one Dash 7 to the next.

Painted bright red, with Air Greenland's classic white logo of a star shaped out of spots, the De Havilland Dash 7s were the workhorses of the north. But the cabin wasn't heated, at least not while the passengers were still boarding. I zipped my collar to my chin and curled my small fists inside the cuffs of my jacket, as the leading edge of the storm arrived in Ilulissat. The crew were eager to take off, and I watched as they snapped curt remarks at a group of American tourists bumbling along the aisle, fiddling with bags in overhead lockers, enjoying the moment.

"Please," the stewardess said. "You need to sit down."

"Yeah, yeah, no problem."

The tallest of the men in the group ignored the stewardess as he pressed a soft holdall into the space in the locker.

"We need to take off."

"Why?" he said. "We're ahead of schedule."

"Oh, come on, Hogan," said one of the women in the group. "Just sit down, already."

The man called Hogan turned to look at her, resting his arm on the top of the seat in front of her as she buckled her seatbelt.

"I'll sit just as soon as I'm ready *Georgina*." He grinned as she curled her lips and fiddled with her thick-rimmed glasses.

"The name's *George*, but you know that."

"Of course I do, *Georgina*." He waved away any further comment with a nod to the stewardess. "But these people will just have to wait."

I looked up at the word *people*, wondering if the

American meant the passengers or the crew. Or if he was addressing Greenlanders in general.

"If you'll sit down," the stewardess said, gesturing at the man's seat.

"Where I come from, you'd call me, *Sir*," Hogan said.

He sat down, and I noted the small smile on the woman's lips as her travelling companion was finally seated.

There were seven in the group, and they seemed less distracted by the weather than I imagined tourists would be on their first visit to the Arctic. They dressed appropriately, which also made me wonder how many times they had been to Greenland. But behind the scarves and beneath their fleece hats, each of them seemed to share a certain degree of irritation. But whether it was directed at the weather or each other, was uncertain. I shivered the thought away, slipped my hands out of my cuffs and tightened my seatbelt, as the stewardess made a quick announcement, rattling through three languages.

"Due to turbulence, there will be no refreshments during the flight," she said. "And please, stay in your seats, and do not use the toilet."

"You mean I can't even take a piss?" Hogan said, lifting his head to look at the stewardess. His chair creaked as he leaned back in it.

"No," she said, as the airframe shuddered with the increased pitch of the engines. "No pissing during the flight, *Sir*."

Everyone smiled at that, even the stewardess.

"Fair enough," Hogan said. He turned to laugh

with his friends, catching my eye as he shifted in his seat. "You're a police officer?" he asked.

"Yes," I said.

"So, I guess you're not allowed to piss, either?"

"I guess not."

"That's fair," Hogan said. He nodded once, and then looked forward, tightening his seatbelt as the Dash 7 thundered down the icy runway.

Part 4

We fled from the storm, droning over the black beaches of Qeqertarsuaq, also known as Disko Island. The coastline was hedged with growlers of ice, the black sand hidden by new snow, as if winter knew summer was coming and was unwilling to relinquish its icy grip of the mountains and the land. The sea ice was already patchy, with large floes sliding up the crests of black waves before crashing and splintering into the troughs below. Those passengers who did not mind the storm pressed their faces to the square windows, exchanging looks and letting go of their seats to point during the brief lulls in the waves of turbulence.

The American, Hogan, was not one of them. I watched as he gripped the arms of his chair, muttering under his breath. I was too far away to hear if he was cursing or praying, but as we flew from one turbulent patch of air into another, I didn't think there was much of a difference.

The captain's voice crackled through the speakers and into the cabin. She apologised for the rough weather, explaining how the early start had perhaps not been early enough to escape the storm.

"But the good news," she said, forcing a measure of optimism into her voice, "is that the helicopter is still flying from mainland Qaarsut to the island of Uummannaq. Until further notice, at least."

I looked out of the window at the ice crystals puckering the glass but chose not to say anything. As selfish as it might sound, I wanted to be on the first helicopter to Uummannaq, preferring to be stranded on the island, than in the settlement of Qaarsut.

The captain prepared us for a bumpy landing, and an even bumpier approach, as she dropped the plane into the leeward side of the mountains, hugging the glaciers tonguing their way down the steep granite sides to the black waters of the fjord below. She curved the Dash 7 in a bumpy arc to land into the wind, finding the balance between dipping and lifting the nose to put air under the wings. The chairs around me creaked, and I wondered if the faux leather covering on the seats, and the arms, could cope with the press of nails from anxious fingers. We landed shortly after, and for once I clapped along with the other passengers in praise of a difficult landing smoothly executed.

As soon as the captain parked the aircraft in front of the airport, I was up and in the aisle, making the most of my lack of luggage and, if I was truthful, exercising a little of my police authority to be the first off the Dash and the first into the helicopter. I forgot all about the Americans as I fastened my seatbelt on the bucket seat inside the helicopter, before reaching up to grab a pair of ear defenders for the short flight to the island. The pilot lifted off and into the wind just a few minutes after the last of the passengers was seated.

Chief of Police Torben Simonsen met me at the heliport. His sharp reputation was softer than I expected, as he waved me into the warmth of the dark blue police Toyota, before driving the short distance to Hotel Asiaq, built onto a low ridge of granite overlooking the harbour.

"You might need some things," he said, after asking about my luggage.

I smiled at the thought of *roughing it* in Qaanaaq, how that experience had changed me. Then I patted my pockets, and said, "I have everything I need."

"Enough for a few days? They say the storm will last until at least the end of the week."

"I'll be fine."

"Well, I've got you in the hotel until then. I called Nuuk and spoke with your Sergeant Duneq." Simonsen glanced at me as if to gauge my reaction before continuing. "There was no rush, you know? Iinta, the guy you're supposed to escort to Nuuk, is no problem, when he behaves. We could have kept him another week."

I looked at Simonsen. We had only ever spoken over the phone, and he was older and greyer than I imagined. He was also Danish, one of a number of Danish policemen who had married a Greenlander, turning a summer position into a permanent one. It reminded me of Constable Kuno Schmidt, and I wondered what he was planning to do once his latest temporary position was over.

"Constable?" Simonsen said, as he parked outside the hotel.

"Yes?"

"I lost you for a moment. I was talking about Duneq."

"Sorry," I said. "Duneq's my supervisor. He likes to keep me busy, and, apparently, as far away from Nuuk as possible."

Simonsen turned in his seat. He tapped a cigarette out of its packet as he leaned his shoulder against the window. "Why?" he asked, as he pinched the cigarette between his lips. "What have you done to piss him off?"

"Nothing," I said, only to add, "Everything. Probably."

Simonsen tapped a packet of matches on his thigh as he waited for me to continue. The unlit cigarette wavered slightly between his lips with each breath.

"He might be jealous, or angry at me. It's a little hard to know."

"Because…"

"Because the commissioner gave me a desk and a phone and told me to take care of the missing persons cases."

"Cases?" Simonsen frowned. "Aren't missing persons just a part of regular police work?"

"Yes," I said. "But every now and again someone calls my phone, and the commissioner encourages me to respond."

"You're a constable."

"Yes."

"Newly trained."

"I nodded."

"And you have a desk." Simonsen plucked the cigarette from his lips and laughed. "Perfect. I can just picture George's face, every time that phone rings."

"Twice," I said, once Simonsen stopped laughing.

"What's that?"

"There's been two calls, since I was given it. Although, there's a good chance people have called the number before, but no one has ever answered. Until now."

"Until *you*," Simonsen said. He opened the door a crack, then lit his cigarette in the shelter of the cab before getting out of the car. "Let's get you checked in, then I can go home for the evening." Smoke chuckled out of his mouth as he took his first drag on the cigarette, before making another comment about Duneq. "Missing persons cases, eh?" he said, as we walked to the hotel door.

"Yes."

Simonsen took a couple of long drags on his cigarette, extinguished it between his finger and thumb, then opened the door. I corralled my hair as he waved me inside, before greeting the young woman waiting behind the tall reception desk.

"Welcome to Hotel Asiaq," she said. "My name is Niinu Kilimii. How can I help you?"

I liked her already, and even more so when she smiled and said that I was lucky, the helicopter made just two flights from Qaarsut before being grounded at the heliport.

"You could have been stuck in Qaarsut," she said.

"Yes," I said, allowing myself the briefest of smiles at my good fortune. "I'm very lucky."

Part 5

Niinu clacked long, false nails over the keyboard of the hotel computer. They fascinated me, and I flexed my hand to look at my own nails, bitten to within a millimetre of the cuticle. I was too lazy for my nail biting to become a habit, rather I bit them when I noticed them snagging on my jacket zipper or catching wayward strands of my hair as I tucked them behind my ears. Atii was the first to lament not having long nails when we found a rare evening to spend clubbing in Nuuk. There was only one club, but plenty of DJs, and we convinced ourselves that we were *clubbing*, and that we were training for New York, London, maybe even Paris.

"But we'll need longer nails," Atii had said, one night when we were practicing our winged eyeliner. "False ones," she said. "So we can take them off for work."

I laughed at the memory, curious at just how practical we had become in an effort to balance our careers with our personal lives. Niinu heard me laugh and pushed back from the computer desk to find the key to my room. She moved a power screwdriver to one side as she plucked my key from a rack.

"Actually," she said, as she pressed the key into my hand. "You're doubly lucky."

"How so?"

Niinu pointed at a group photo on the wall behind her desk. A younger and slighter Niinu posed in the front of a group of tourists. "They came two years ago, and are due to arrive on the next helicopter," she said, as she leaned on the counter. "They've taken six double rooms, leaving just one unoccupied." Niinu tapped the key in my hand. "We have twenty rooms, but the rest are being refurbished. My *ataata*, the janitor, is very busy."

"Your dad works here too?"

"As did my *anaana*," Niinu said. "Before she died."

"I'm sorry," I said.

"Not your fault. She was sick – too much to drink. Then one night, she fell asleep outside." Niinu shrugged. "It was winter. She died just four metres from the front door."

I caught her eye for just a second, seeing the grief welling there before she turned back to the photo.

"There used to be seven in the group, but one of the men went missing two years ago." Niinu reached out to press the tip of one of her long nails on the face of a short man standing beside her in the photo. "His name was Justin Moon. He was very kind." Niinu looked away for a moment, as if to catch her breath.

"And they're coming back?"

"*Aap*," Niinu said. "They were on the second helicopter to leave Qaarsut. If they hadn't made it, you would have had the whole hotel to yourself."

27

Niinu paused to look past me as a pair of bright headlights cut through the snow and lit up the reception area. "Here they come now."

I raised my hand to shield my eyes, recognising a few of the passengers who had flown with me from Ilulissat, including the tall man called Hogan, and the woman he called Georgina.

"You're going to be busy checking them in," I said, lowering my hand. "I'll leave you to it."

"Dinner's at seven," Niinu said, as I climbed the steep staircase to the first floor; I could almost see the sheer wall of granite beneath the foundations with each step.

"Thanks," I said.

I found my room at the top of the stairs, the first on the right along a narrow corridor. The Americans bustled through the front door as I turned the key in the lock. I could still hear them as I closed the door and flopped onto the bed. While Hotel Asiaq didn't have the same number of stars as the bigger hotels in Ilulissat, it was, at least, warm and cosy, if not luxurious. The bed was harder than I was used to, and something heavy – shutters or perhaps a door – was banging in the wind. I closed my eyes for a moment, wishing that the few essentials I had packed included earplugs.

I rolled off the bed and onto my feet when my utility belt started to bother me. I curled it onto the desk, then placed my pistol and two spare magazines in the safe. I checked my phone, and realised I had an hour before dinner. Simonsen said I was his last job before he finished for the day, and I was far enough from Nuuk to escape Sergeant

Duneq's clutches.

"I have the evening off," I said, as I plugged my phone into its charger.

The storm whipped itself into a frenzy outside, scratching the window with needles of ice. The banging continued with a regularity that I knew would keep me awake the whole night, but I discovered that the bathroom was better insulated, and I shrugged off my uniform to take a shower. I didn't have a change of clothes, but I could at least try to dress for dinner. I amused myself with the various ways I could make the light blue shirt of my uniform at least a tiny bit more casual, only to shriek and forget all about it under the first burst of cold water from the shower. It seemed I wasn't the only one freshening up before dinner.

Part 6

It struck me, as I climbed down the stairs for dinner, that the man in the photo had gone missing, but I had not asked *where*. I pushed the thought to one side as the noise from the dining room breached the swing door. I paused before entering, fixing my damp hair into a ponytail, tucking my shirt into my cargo trousers, and affecting as casual a look as I could before dinner. Technically I was off duty, but a police officer is never off, and definitely not when they are still in uniform. It was all still new to me, and Sergeant Duneq hadn't exactly been forthcoming with the grey areas of police work. I think he preferred that I stumble upon them all by myself. I took a breath, pushed the door open, and stepped into the dining room.

"Constable," the man called Hogan said, as I walked to an empty table by the window. "Join us, please."

"Yes, do," said the woman sitting beside him. She tugged at the empty chair next to her, gesturing for me to sit down once she had pulled it out from under the table. "You must join us," she said, as I started to protest. "You can put us girls in the majority for once."

I glanced at the table, blushing under the sudden scrutiny of six strangers, but noting at the same time that the sexes were evenly represented.

"If you're sure?" I said.

"Sure?" Hogan laughed as he reached for the bottle of wine. "*Sure,* we're sure," he said, as he filled a spare glass to the brim. He handed it to me as soon as I sat down. "Unless you're on duty?"

"Sort of," I said, without really being sure. I took a sip as they started the introductions.

"I'm Jordan Carmichaels," said the woman beside me. "I'm a dietician, but you just eat whatever you like, honey, I'm on holiday."

"Which is just as well," Hogan said. "Otherwise she'd be charging by the hour."

"Ignore him," Jordan said. She placed a cool and jewelled hand on mine as she pointed a slender finger at the rest of the group in turn. "Opposite you is Bradley…"

"Washington," the man said, extending his hand across to the table.

I shook it awkwardly with my left hand as Jordan refused to release my right. Greenland has such a small population, with a proportionate diversity. Although Greenland swelled with tourists each summer, Bradley was one of the few black men I had met in person. He smiled at my awkward handshake, before dipping his head towards Jordan as if he understood she was never letting go.

"I'm a contractor," he said, as he let go of my hand.

"What kind?" I asked.

"He builds condos, honey," Jordan said. "Terribly boring."

"But lucrative," Bradley said.

"Of course it is," Hogan said, reaching for the wine. "Especially when they burn down, and you reap the..."

"Hogan!" Jordan said. She patted my hand. "Just ignore him, honey."

Hogan seemed to be the life of the party, or at least, the loudest among them. He was difficult to ignore, and even more so in his loud Hawaiian shirt. My uniform blues paled in comparison. But I wasn't the only one wearing a uniform of sorts. The man sitting beside Hogan wore what looked like a one-piece sleeping suit.

"That's Mosaic," Jordan said, lowering her voice as she pointed at the slim man in the one-piece. "He's our celebrity."

"I can hear you, Jordan," Mosaic said. He wrapped his thin fingers around a tall wine glass, extending his little finger as he took a sip. "Just because *you* don't approve."

"Some of us work for a living," Jordan said. "That's all."

"I work."

"Mosaic, you dear, sweet thing." Jordan lifted her finger, cutting him off as he started to speak. "*YouTubing* is not working. Let's not fight about this again."

"I'm not fighting. I never fight, *Jordan*," Mosaic said. He turned his hand to point his little finger at her. "You start it, every time. Always you. And especially in front of strangers."

Mosaic looked at me, and I blushed again, wishing I had taken the table by the window.

"The Constable..." Jordan paused to squeeze

my hand. "What's your name, honey? We can't call you *Constable* all evening."

"Petra," I said.

"Petra? Such a lovely name." Jordan smiled, before turning back to Mosaic. "Petra is hardly a stranger. *We* are the strangers. This is *her* country, after all."

"And yet here we are, again."

I turned to look at the woman sitting beside Bradley, noting her strong hands, and the square cut of her jaw.

"Let's not get into that," Jordan said.

The woman gave Jordan a look, and I felt the slightest shift in Jordan's grip on my hand, as if the look unsettled her.

"This is Claudia," Jordan said. She let go of my hand to reach for a glass of water.

"Claudia Nickel," the woman said. "Carpenter."

"And I'm a dentist," Hogan said. The table wobbled as he reached across it to shake my hand. "Hogan Mayflower, like the ship," he said.

"The ship?" I said, once he let go of my hand.

"Yes, *the* ship, the pilgrims' ship." He turned to the woman he called Georgina for support. "She doesn't know the ship."

"Not everyone has to know our history," Georgina said. "Do you know the history of Greenland, Hogan?"

"Tiny country, with a population that can fit inside a stadium – why should I?"

"My point, exactly," Georgina said. She turned to me and smiled. "As Jordan said, you should probably just ignore Hogan. God knows we try to."

"And what do you do?" I asked, keen to keep the conversation going, if only to avoid having to talk about Greenland's history, or the *Mayflower*'s.

"I'm a veterinarian," she said. "Which makes me wonder, what can you tell me about the dogs?"

"Dogs?"

"Yes, the sledge dogs." Georgina made a brief sweeping gesture with her hand that seemed to encompass the whole island. "Dotted about the rocks, running free…"

"They're everywhere," Mosaic said.

"Right," Jordan said. "You're a dog person now?"

"Friends," Bradley said. He cleared his throat, then paused to answer a call on his mobile, thumbing the screen to end it as soon as he saw the number. "A toast." The table hushed as everyone reached for their glass. I lifted mine, casting another longing glance at the empty table by the window. "To our new friend, Petra," he said, with a nod in my direction. "And to Justin, our long-lost and sorely missed friend."

"Justin," everyone said, before taking long sips of white or red wine.

"Maybe one day we'll finally discover what happened to him," Bradley said, as he set his wine glass on the table.

"Why not," Hogan said.

"Why not *what*, Hogan?" Jordan said.

"Let's find out what happened to him."

"How?"

"Isn't it obvious?" Hogan pushed his seat back and stood up. "Look," he said, gesturing at me. "We have a detective among us."

"I'm just a constable," I said, only to be drowned out by another burst of Hogan's enthusiasm.

"And the storm," he said, as he walked to window. "It's perfect. Don't you see?"

"See what?" Bradley said.

"That all the pieces of the puzzle are here." Hogan straightened both arms and pointed at the table. "Justin went missing here, and we've been coming back all these years, just hoping there might be a shred of a clue that might tell us what happened." He pointed at the window. "It was a night just like this one. A storm – maybe even stronger and colder than this. I don't remember. But if she can help us, guide us through it."

"Me?" I said, pressing a quick-bitten finger to my chest.

"Yes, Detective. You."

"I don't…"

"Never mind that," he said, waving his hand. "If everyone agrees, then that's what we'll do, now, this very evening. Right after dinner."

"Do what, exactly?" Jordan asked.

"Find Justin's killer."

I swore beneath my breath as the table erupted in curses and accusations. Words such as *stupid* and *immature* crossed back and forth, together with *insensitive* and a longer tirade from Jordan appealing for everyone to calm down and to just ignore Hogan.

The problem was, I couldn't, but it had less to do with being a police officer, and far more to do with my own curiosity. Why would else would six barely amicable adults return to the last place they had seen their friend if not to find answers? Perhaps my dinner attire was appropriate after all.

"I'll do it," I said.

"What?" Jordan waved her hands, shushing everyone until she was the only one speaking. "What did you say, honey?"

"I said I'll do it. I'll help you."

"See?" Hogan clapped his hands together. "Perfect. We'll start straight after dinner."

Part 7

Hotel Asiaq had a study, although the name of the room was perhaps grander than the room itself. The mahogany veneer panels screwed into the walls, together with a classic American library style lamp, complete with brass fittings and a jade shade, added a touch of old-world class, wholly out of place in Greenland, but not unpleasant. The floorboards creaked as I squeezed around the desk, and the ornaments on the shelves – *Tupilaq* carved out of narwhal teeth and whale bone – rattled within a millimetre of toppling. The dust on the shelves suggested that few people visited the study, but it was perfect for my purpose.

"What are you going to do?" Niinu asked.

"I'm going to help the group discover what happened to their friend – the one you showed me in the photo."

"And why... I mean *how* are you going to do that?"

"By asking lots of questions."

"Is this a case then?" Niinu's forehead creased as she frowned.

"Not really," I said, wondering how I should describe it. "I suppose you could call it evening entertainment."

"Oh," Niinu said. "That's better."

"Why?"

"Because I don't think the Chief would be happy if you were investigating. *Ataata* said he was quite frustrated."

"Because they never found Justin?"

"*Aap*. It was the month of May and we still had sea ice, so there were no boats on the water. The ice was getting thin, and the police had just said we couldn't drive on it anymore. Then Justin disappeared, and the Chief was pissed off that he might have gone for a walk. They had hunters out searching the ice, and then the Chief sent one of his officers up the mountain." Niinu turned to point in the direction of the heart-shaped mountain that loomed over the town of Uummannaq.

"But they didn't find any clues?"

Niinu shook her head.

"Not a trace?"

"Nothing."

The fine hairs on my arms prickled with a surge of excitement as I teased at Niinu's memory of what happened to Justin Moon. I didn't want to step on Simonsen's toes, but as long as the case was nothing more than entertainment, a way to pass the time during the storm, I decided that I could go ahead. I tugged my smartphone out of my pocket and slid it onto the desk.

The study was tucked into a corner of the hotel, close to the kitchen. I wouldn't have been surprised if it used to be a pantry, before being remodelled as a feature for the hotel. Once Niinu had gone, and if I didn't move, the study was silent, but the storm outside sifted snow along the outer walls like sand,

and from somewhere outside, I could hear the same shutter banging in the wind.

I looked up as Jordan knocked on the door.

"Can I come in?"

"Yes, of course," I said.

Jordan took a moment to glance around the study, turning her head to the bone figures as they rattled on the bookshelves.

"I just wanted to ask if you're okay with this?"

"I am," I said.

"Only, Hogan can be so bullish at times. Some people find it hard to say no to him."

"It's okay. Really."

Jordan cupped her hands in front of her, resting them just above the slim belt of her jeans. She turned the largest of her rings on her left hand with the little finger of her right, turning the ring back and forth as she looked at me.

"Was there something else?" I asked. "Would you rather I didn't do this?"

"What?"

"Am I being insensitive?"

My excitement diminished as I realised I probably was. The combination of being stranded by bad weather, trapped in a hotel on a remote island, and presented with a true missing persons case had diluted my better judgement. I thought briefly of Tuukula, almost expecting him to appear in the doorway, teasing me with a knowing smile, waiting for me to come to my own conclusion about my next step, or the best course of action.

"No, of course not. Everything is fine," Jordan said. "It's all fine, honey." She paused to look at her hands, then held them by her sides, as if suddenly self-conscious about her ring-turning. "To be honest, I think we all want to know what happened to Justin, but…" She laughed. "You saw us at dinner. We're not good at talking. We're far too combative, I think."

"But you want to know what happened to Justin?"

"Yes. Absolutely. That's why we came back."

Jordan looked at me for a moment, then looked away, before excusing herself, and promising to send someone in to begin.

"Who would you like, first?" she asked.

I hadn't thought about it.

"How about Hogan?" Jordan said. "After all, he started it. He might as well go first."

"That's fine," I said. "I'll find a second chair."

Jordan nodded, then slipped out of the study. I followed her out, stopping in the dining room to find another chair. When I returned, I found Hogan sitting behind the desk.

"So, Detective," he said, lacing his fingers behind his head. "Shall we begin?"

Part 8

"Justin was an ass," Hogan said. He spun my smartphone on the desk between us, drawing my attention to his thick fingers, and making me wonder how a dentist with such big hands could do work inside small mouths. Hogan, however, had a big mouth, and lots of opinions. I said nothing. I just let him speak.

"Don't get me wrong, he was a great guy, but he was a real pain in the ass." Hogan stopped spinning my phone and leaned back in the chair. He ran his thick fingers through his greasy blond hair a couple of times before continuing. "Everybody loved him, of course we did. But he had this way about him, no matter how you talked with him, he just had this kind of expectant manner. I don't know how to describe it, but he would pause – you know? He'd say something and then pause, as if you had to fill in the blank. Like he *expected* you to do it. I guess it had something to do with his job. He was an insurance broker. Did I mention that?"

"No."

"He was good at it. He had a successful business, writing policies to fit people's needs, and I mean exactly. Say you had an expensive watch."

Hogan reached forward, pressing his hand close to my face and turning it so that I could see the big gold watch on his wrist. He pulled it back and wiped a speck of imaginary dust from the face.

"You have something like this, you want to insure it, believe me. But Justin could write a policy that was so specific, tailor-made, if you know what I mean?"

"Yes," I said, but it was unnecessary. Hogan continued without even glancing at me.

"So, this watch – I know it has a dodgy winder. Too thin for my fingers. So, I asked Justin if he could write a policy that allowed me to claim for the watch, if it was stolen, or broken, but also to claim for the winder. It breaks all the time, but the deductible – you know, what you pay before the insurance coverage kicks in?"

I nodded.

"Well, Justin wrote a policy that covered the winder. I mean, I'm breaking it all the time. So, he does one of his expectant pauses, like I just told you about, and he waits, and I ask him if he could write me something that lets me claim on the winder? I love this watch. It was my grandfather's. But if I had to pay to get it fixed every time the winder broke; I may as well buy a new watch. Justin helped me out with that. Sure, the premium is a little higher, but the number of times I break the winder... Let's just say it works out for me in the end. He did the same thing with policies for my practice." Hogan paused. "And George's dog."

"George?"

"Yeah, Georgina. She likes to be called George. I think it's because she's from the east coast, New York state."

"But you call her Georgina," I said.

"Sure, to her face. That's right. But, hey, it's just you and me, Detective."

Hogan grinned and added one of what he might describe as Justin's expectant pauses. I filled it with a question about George – or Georgina's – dog.

"What kind of policy?"

"For her dog?" Hogan nodded once more. "She's got an Afghan. It sheds," he said, shaking his hand. "It sheds so much, it's like it's got a disease or something. So George insured the dog's fur. I mean, that's how good Justin was. You'd think brokers would write an insurance policy for anything. But that's just a load of bull. But Justin? He actually did it." Hogan paused to take a long breath. "He insured everything. I guess that, at the end, he might have insured too much."

"I don't understand," I said. "How could he insure too much?"

"Did I say that?" Hogan glanced at my phone.

"Yes."

"Right, okay. Maybe someone asked him to insure something he shouldn't have. What do I know? You'd have to ask the others."

Hogan rested his hands in his lap, then looked away, commenting on the ugly faces of the *Tupilaq* on the shelves as I puzzled over what he had said about insurances. I decided to leave it and return to the basic details I needed to piece together the events surrounding Justin's disappearance.

"Justin went missing two years ago," I said. "What happened that night?"

"You mean what do I remember?"

"Yes, whatever you can. Anything will help. And if you know what you told the police…"

"The police?"

"Yes," I said. I could feel what Atii called my curious frown pinching the skin just above my nose. "The chief of police, Simonsen. Niinu told me he organised a search."

"For Justin?"

"Yes."

"I don't remember anyone doing any searching." Hogan shook his head. "Justin just disappeared. He was at dinner. He sat next to Mosaic, I think. They talked. We all talked. We all drank a bit – maybe too much. It was the last night before we flew the following morning."

"And the next morning?"

"I had a really thick head. A hangover, you know?"

"Yes," I said. I knew all about hangovers, but the way Hogan fidgeted on the chair as he talked was far more interesting.

"We got a ride to the heliport. I remember asking where Justin was. It was me who asked," he said, leaning close to my phone. "But no one had seen him at breakfast. And then we had to go."

"So, you just left him?"

"Hey, we're all adults here. It's not like we're family. Sure, someone must have knocked on his door. Maybe Jordan. I don't know. But then we had to go, and you know what it's like. When the weather is right, you just have to go. You can't wait around. It might be sunny one minute, and a real storm the next." He turned in his seat, looking for a window, only to point at the bookshelf when he realised there wasn't one.

"You left together?"

"In the hotel car. Two trips."

"Without Justin?"

"Hey, I asked where he was. If anyone had seen him. Then we just had to go."

"And the last time you saw him?"

"He was sitting next to Claudia at dinner."

"Claudia?"

"That's right." Hogan pointed at my phone. "Check your recording. That's what I said."

It wasn't, and he knew it. But before I could quiz him about it, he pushed back his chair and walked out of the study.

Part 9

As Hogan left the study, the wind outside filled the void, together with the flap and bang of the shutter somewhere below the study. The hotel was built on thick wooden stilts on top of the rocks, just like all the houses on the island. Some of the houses had plywood sheets screwed into the stilts to make a cellar of sorts, albeit of various sizes and degrees of functionality. Mostly, it was to improve the aesthetic look of a house. In the case of the hotel, the name was painted in large white letters along the plywood façade facing the harbour. Access to the Arctic cellars was often through a small door or hatch, and I could just imagine that the wind had teased one of the hatches open. I thought about looking for it, but Mosaic stopped me as I stood up to leave the study.

"You're leaving?" he said. "I can come back."

"No, it's fine," I said, gesturing to the seat Hogan had just vacated. "Please sit down."

"I suppose you want to know all about me?" Mosaic said.

I waited for him to sit down, intrigued by the way he brushed the seat of the chair with the cuff of his shirt before sitting.

"A little, I guess," I said.

"You don't have *YouTube* in Greenland? Is it

blocked?" Mosaic leaned over the desk as I started a new recording. "Are you living under an oppressive regime?" he whispered.

"Greenland is a democracy," I said, wrangling the smile from my lips.

"Sure, I knew that, but you hear all kinds of things. And I just wanted to be sure you were okay."

I felt the brush of soft cotton on my skin as Mosaic reached out to pat my hand. His fingers were hidden inside his cuffs.

"If you could just tell me about your relationship to Justin. How you knew him. Maybe how you met."

"How we met?" Mosaic smiled, flashing a set of perfect teeth. "He insured my teeth. And in my work, *that's* a serious investment. Oh, sure, you can do wonders with lighting and editing. But video is just one medium. I like to meet people."

"And is Hogan your dentist?"

"That pig?" Mosaic sneered. "God no. I wouldn't trust him to work on a mannequin. Have you seen his hands?"

"Yes," I said, wondering if I shouldn't have said anything at all.

"Never mind that. Justin insured my teeth. He put me in touch with Jordan. She told me what to eat, so that I wouldn't colour my teeth. You noticed I drank the white wine, not the red? Just like I don't drink coffee or tea."

"But at dinner, I got the impression that you and Jordan…"

"We're on a break," he said. "Too much of a

good thing, I think. We need a pause. That's all."

"And Justin?"

"That night, two years ago, everything changed."

I caught a glimpse of Mosaic's hands as he rested his elbows on the table and propped his chin between laced fingers. Unlike my lazy approach to biting nails, it seemed that Mosaic was a connoisseur, and that he chose his long-cuffed shirts with care. But as he recalled the last night he had seen Justin, it seemed that the insurance broker's disappearance was of greater concern than revealing the quicks of his fingers.

"I liked Justin," he said. "And he knew it."

"You had a relationship with him?"

"Oh, please," Mosaic said, with a shake of his head. "I said I liked him, but I was never going to *love* him. You understand?"

"I think so."

"Justin *loved* everybody. And I just didn't have the time for that kind of thing. I let him know that I was available, but that I wasn't going to wait, and that he would have to stop sleeping around if he wanted to have anything, and I mean *anything* to do with me."

Mosaic slipped his fingers back inside his cuffs as he leaned back in his chair.

"Was Justin in a relationship?" I asked. "With any of the others in your group?"

"Our *group*?" Mosaic laughed. "It's not like we're a band. We don't *group*. Although, Justin had his groupies. Just ask Bradley."

"Justin had a relationship with Bradley?"

"I didn't say that. But if I did say that, or if I was saying anything like that, I would say that you had to ask Bradley where he was the night Justin disappeared. That's all I'm saying."

"Where were you the night he disappeared?"

"Me?" Mosaic shrugged. "I was at dinner. Then I took a walk with Jordan – you can ask her."

"I thought there was a storm?"

"Oh, sure," he said. "We just took a short walk, just outside the door really. One last cigarette."

"Cigarettes stain your teeth," I said, feeling another pinch of curiosity above my nose.

"You've got a smart mouth, Detective." Mosaic's lips curled as he spoke. "But sure, you're right. That's why it was our *last* cigarette." He paused to point at my phone. "Are you recording this?"

"Yes."

"Then you'll have to sign something – a disclaimer. I sell everything. My image, my voice. I'll need a chit to prove you won't try and sell that."

"It's just for my notes."

"Whatever. I'll still need a chit."

Mosaic stood up and walked to the door. I stopped him with a last question.

"Did you knock on Justin's door, the next morning?"

"What?"

"You had to be at the heliport. I understand the hotel car was going to take you."

"And?"

"You were leaving as a group. If Justin wasn't there…"

"Oh, sure, I knocked on his door." Mosaic shrugged. "He said he was getting ready, and that we should just go on without him."

"What time did he say that?"

"The time?" Mosaic lifted his hands and let his cuffs roll down his pale arms. "I don't wear a watch," he said, letting his hands fall to his sides. "But it was after breakfast. That I remember." He took a last glance at my phone, and said, "I'll still need that chit."

Part 10

My head buzzed with Hogan and Mosaic's slightly different account – just enough to confuse me, with plenty to pique my interest. It seemed strange that at least two of the group were unaware that the police had searched for Justin Moon on the day they left the island. Even more curious, was the fact that although they professed to be friends, they showed little sympathy when he missed his flights – the helicopter to the mainland, and the fixed-wing flying south for their connecting flight home.

But why Greenland?

Tourists rarely came more than once to Greenland, the cost of flights, food and accommodation were prohibitive. But seven Americans visited Greenland, and the same group came back two years following the death of one of their group. It seemed clear to me that finding a motive for their visit was crucial to understanding how or why Justin might disappear.

I thought of Atii and wished she were with me, although mysteries had never been her thing.

"Mysteries are for lawyers," she once said during training. "I don't mind gathering information and passing it on, but when I go home at night, I just want to relax, not sit on the couch or lie in bed thinking about stuff. Life's too short for that."

I needed help.

I thumbed the screen of my smartphone to check the time, cursing as I realised it was getting later and later. Simonsen would be home now, and I could hardly disturb him with an emergency, since the missing person had been missing for two years. It would have to wait until morning.

"But I need a break," I said, as I walked out of the study.

The man leaning against the counter in the hotel reception was tall enough to give Sergeant Gaba Alatak a run for his money. I hadn't thought of Gaba for a while – I tried not to. It was hard enough listening to Atii's tales of romantic conquests with the leader of the police Special Response Unit, but, regardless, stray thoughts of Gaba popped into my head whenever I least expected, often prompted by the least expected things.

Like the man in reception.

"Juuliu," he said, offering his hand as I approached. "I'm Niinu's *ataata*." His Danish was flawless, surprising me, as he nodded at the empty chair in front of the computer. "I'm just waiting for her."

"You're the janitor."

"*Aap*," he said. His bushy black eyebrows wriggled as he smiled.

"There's something banging outside," I said.

Juuliu nodded. "I know, but I haven't found it yet."

"I think it's a shutter, or something."

Juuliu reached over the counter to pick up the power screwdriver I had seen earlier. "And when I find it, I'm going to fix it," he said.

"Now?"

"*Imaqa*." He shrugged, and then looked at his watch. "It's late. Maybe it will blow off in the storm. Then I don't have to fix it."

There was a certain logic to that, and I nodded that it could wait.

"Unless you want to go out and look?"

"Outside?"

"*Aap*," he said. "You look like you need some air."

"Yes," I said. "But I'll need my jacket."

Juuliu moved away from the counter and ducked beneath an arch leading to the kitchen. He returned with a huge *Canada Goose* down jacket, with a fur-lined hood.

"It's Niinu's," he said. "You can borrow it."

"Thanks," I said, as I slipped my arms into the sleeves, and then zipped the jacket all the way to top of the collar. The fur tickled my forehead, and I adjusted the strap at the back of the hood to lift it a little.

"Are we done already?"

I turned my head to one side, looking for whoever spoke, only to have Juuliu grasp my shoulders and turn me back again until I was facing Bradley Washington. Both men were taller than me, and I lifted my chin to look up.

"Mosaic said you were ready for me."

"Yes," I said.

"She's having a break," Juuliu said, surprising me for a second time with his English. "We'll be back soon."

Juuliu steered me towards the front door. I tried to adjust the hood again but gave up in a fit of giggles as I bumped into the glass window beside the door.

"This way," Juuliu said.

"I can't see," I said.

"*Aap*. I know."

We left Bradley in the reception. I might have thought about his reaction, perhaps even promised that I would be back soon, but the wind buffeted me across the icy ground outside the hotel, and the cold choked the breath out of my lungs. Juuliu bent his arm and I hooked my hand around it, following his lead as we slid across the ice and stomped in the snow around the side of the hotel.

I let Juuliu lead as I concentrated my efforts on dipping my head and placing my feet. I bumped into him as he stopped, and then looked up when he tapped my shoulder.

"There," he said, jabbing his bare fingers at a square door banging in the wind.

"Are you going to screw it shut?" I said, shouting into the wind.

"*Aap*."

I let go of Juuliu as he fiddled with the screwdriver in his hands. He cursed as he dropped several long screws into the snow at his feet, and again when he realised the battery was empty.

"I have another battery inside," he said, pressing his face close to my hood. "Do you want to come back with me?"

A gust of icy wind pushed me off balance, and I gripped Juuliu's arm, steadying myself before replying.

"I'll wait here," I said, then pointed at the cellar door. "I'll wait inside."

"You're sure?"

"Yes," I said.

Juuliu nodded once, and then slipped away. I watched him follow the path through the rocks back to the corner of the hotel. As soon as he was gone, I reached for the door, holding it as I peered into the cellar inside. There was a flashlight on my utility belt, and I sighed at the thought of going back to my room to fetch it. But as I peered into the cellar, I noticed a dim light creeping around the corners of more plywood sheets deeper inside the cellar, as if there were two cellars, one inside the other.

The choice was easy. I could stay outside and freeze, or I could crawl inside the cellar and wait for Juuliu to return. The third option of walking back to the hotel didn't even occur to me, I was too curious to leave without at least taking a quick look and checking out the light.

I took a moment to hitch the tails of Niinu's long coat up to my waist, folding and bunching the coat until it was more like a jacket. I cinched the draw cords tight before lifting one leg up and then through the cellar entrance. The door flapped against my shoulder and I worried that a rusty nail might rip Niinu's jacket. But with one leg already inside, I was committed. I crawled the rest of the way in and paused to let my eyes adjust to the dark.

The rocks inside were dusted with snow, and at the back of cellar, lit by the soft glow of light creeping around the sheets of plywood, was a row of three wooden coffins.

Part 11

In any other country, coffins hidden beneath a hotel might have raised alarm bells, if they had been discovered. But in Greenland, an empty coffin was an empty vessel, something to be used. The square door cut into the plywood sheets that created the cellar was too small for the coffins to be removed. So, if they couldn't be used for their original purpose, and they couldn't be moved without breaking them apart, then the only logical thing to be done with them was to use them for storage. Somebody had done just that, sliding the lids to one side to make room for tins of paint inside. I smiled at the practical use of the coffins, before taking a closer look at the plywood sheets boxing the smaller room inside the cellar, out of which a creamy yellow light shone between the joins.

The bottom section of each plywood sheet had been cut like a jigsaw puzzle to accommodate the irregular peaks and mounds of the granite upon which the hotel was built. The sheets were screwed into the thick stilts supporting the hotel above my head. I slipped my hand beneath one ragged edge of plywood and turned it in the light, tilting my head to one side to see around my breath crystallising in the chill cellar air. Niinu's long jacket was surprisingly warm, and the wind did little more than funnel tendrils of dry snow into the cellar, like thin powdery fingers reaching in, questing for something to hold onto.

Together with the flapping of the door, and the darkness, barely broken by the thin rectangles of yellow light, the scene was set for a horror movie, and I pulled my hand out of the light. I unfolded the tails of Niinu's jacket down to my knees and felt something stiff crumple inside one of the pockets. I slipped my hand inside and pulled out an envelope, turning it in the available light to read the address and that of the sender, before admonishing myself for intruding on Niinu's privacy, and stuffing the envelope back into Niinu's pocket.

"Found something interesting?" said a deep voice behind me.

The man's voice, the horror setting, and being caught in the act of looking at someone's private correspondence gave me a start, and I spun around, slipping in the snow until I landed on my backside. Bradley's big frame filled the cellar entrance as he squeezed through the square door. I caught my breath as I watched him, wondering how he could fit, and, if he did, how he might get out again.

"I'm guilty," he said, once he was inside the cellar. "Of following you."

"Why did you?"

He jabbed his thumb towards the roof and nodded. "I was ready for my interview, but you took off."

"I was going to come back."

"I know," he said. "But I was curious, and now we're here I'm even more curious." He pointed to his left. "Are those coffins?"

"Yes," I said.

"Empty?"

"No." Bradley started to shiver as I smiled. "They're full of paint pots and stuff."

"Paint?"

"Yes."

Bradley clenched his fists as he began to shake. "What else do you know? I mean, what did Hogan and Mosaic tell you?"

"I'm not sure I should say," I said. "At least not yet." Bradley started to shiver in his thin jacket and even thinner jeans. "Perhaps we should go. You look cold."

I stood up and took a step towards the square door banging in the wind. Bradley moved to block my path.

"First," he said, teeth clacking. "Tell me what the others said."

"Bradley…"

"Tell me," he said.

He raised his arm, holding out a massive hand as if to push me deeper into the cellar. He lowered it again to wrap his arms around his chest.

"Do I have to remind you I'm a police officer?" I said, but he seemed distracted.

"What's that light?" he asked, looking around me. "What's inside that room?"

"I don't know."

"Those panels have been moved." Bradley shuffled forward to take a closer look at the snow drifting up and beneath the bottom of the panels. "Sawdust in the snow," he said, before pointing at the large flathead screws drilled into the edges of the panels in neat rows. "It's recent. They've been screwed in and out, since it started snowing."

I followed the direction in which Bradley was pointing, wishing for the second time that I had my flashlight. But a closer inspection revealed sawdust sprinkled on top of and down the fresh drifts of snow that the wind had blown along and up the granite floor. There wasn't much, but enough to suggest that it was new.

"Juuliu will know," I said, as I wondered about footprints. I laughed again as I grasped at assumptions, assuming that the sawdust was significant, that something of interest was hidden behind the panels. But the only recent footprints would be my own, Bradley's and Juuliu's, if he had even been down here. The light could have been on for weeks, depending upon the bulb.

I decided it was nothing of interest. Someone had probably turned a light on somewhere and forgot to turn it off. Old hotels like old houses would be full of strange switches, forgotten each time the building changed hands, only to be discovered again by chance, or during a renovation.

But, perhaps, there was more to this light. Juuliu revealed as much when he returned and poked his head inside the square door, looking at me, before flicking his eyes to the light.

The flicker suggested it was not supposed to be turned on.

I wanted to ask Juuliu about the light and the inner cellar, only to be distracted by Bradley as he started to speak, slurring his words as he removed his jacket, I knew any questions I had would have to wait. Bradley Washington was going hypothermic.

Part 12

"You have to help me, Juuliu," I said, as I struggled to zip Bradley's jacket. Each time I got the zip halfway up his jacket, he brushed my hands away, complaining that he was too hot. "I can't do this by myself."

Juuliu was more interested in the light behind the panels. He crawled into the cellar and worked his way towards the inner room.

"Juuliu," I said, tugging at his jacket sleeve. "Bradley needs our help. We have to get him inside." I paused to look at Bradley, noting the deep purple colour of his lips, and adjusted my plan. "He's too far gone," I said, pulling my smartphone from my pocket. "We need to get him to hospital."

Perhaps it was the word hospital that finally convinced Juuliu that one of the guests needed help. He put the screwdriver down, and nodded that he would help, glancing just one more time at the light before helping me guide Bradley to the hole leading out of the cellar.

I had forgotten about the wind.

The square door caught my head as I crawled out of the cellar, dazing me for a moment until the sharp bite of the wind cleared my head and I held the door to one side as Juuliu pushed Bradley's head and shoulders out of the cellar and into the wind. I took Bradley's hands, reminding myself that he was a building contractor as the strength of his grip surprised me.

He spotted the sawdust.

The thought needled one part of my mind, just like the snow spinning through the wind needled my eyes, splintering upon my cheeks. I let go of Bradley for a second to claw my hair out of my eyes but gave up a second later. We had to get him inside. I could worry about my hair later. Juuliu said something about nailing the door shut, but I convinced him that it could wait.

"We have to get him inside, and then call the ambulance."

I fumbled my phone back into my pocket, deciding that getting Bradley inside was the priority. Juuliu nodded, giving the cellar just one last glance before supporting Bradley on one side, as I held onto the other. Bradley shivered as we staggered along the path to the hotel entrance, dripping nonsense words from his mouth all the way to the door. Niinu stared at us for a moment from behind the desk, before running to the door to open it.

"Call the hospital," I said to Niinu, as we dumped Bradley into the large armchair by the door. "Tell them he's hypothermic."

Niinu nodded and ran back to the desk. As she started to dial, Bradley's companions drifted out of the dining hall into the reception area.

"What's wrong with him?" Hogan asked.

"He's cold," I said.

"He's cold? We're all cold."

"He was outside," I said, curbing my irritation as I focused on Bradley. Juuliu brought blankets from a cupboard set into a recess in the wall, and we wrapped them around Bradley's shoulders.

"What was he doing outside?" Georgina asked, hushing Hogan as he made another quip about how it was supposed to be cold in Greenland. "I thought he was your next interview?"

"He was," I said.

I paused as the ambulance headlights flashed up the steep slope to the hotel entrance. The driver and one of the porters from the hospital climbed out of the ambulance – a white transit – and then grabbed a wheelchair from the back of the van. It might have been comical, and anyone else might have laughed at the sight of two small Greenlandic men trying to stuff a large American man into a tiny wheelchair, but no one laughed. Neither was anyone watching Bradley as the hospital staff wheeled him through the storm to the back of the ambulance. They were all looking at me.

"And?" Georgina asked, as the driver carefully reversed the ambulance down the slope and back onto the road. "Did you?"

"What?"

"Interview him?"

"No," I said.

"But did he say anything to you?"

I don't know what had changed since I interviewed Mosaic, but the banter around the dining table had changed into a palpable tension, sparking between the guests.

"Maybe we should have some coffee," I said,

catching Niinu's eye. "Then I can tell you what I know so far."

"I think that's a good idea," Jordan said, and she ushered everyone back into the dining room. "Let's give her a moment, and then the detective can bring us up to speed."

"Constable," I said, but they were already gone.

Juuliu said something quietly in Greenlandic to his daughter, before closing the cupboard door and excusing himself. I expected him to go outside, to screw the cellar door shut, but instead he walked to the kitchen.

Niinu stared at me, her eyes fixed on the deep pockets of her jacket.

"I'm sorry," I said. "Juuliu said I could borrow it."

Niinu nodded, but her eyes remained fixed on the pockets.

"I found something. And I'm sorry, but I bent it a little." I tugged the envelope out of the jacket and pressed it into Niinu's hands. "I hope it wasn't important."

"It's just a letter," Niinu said, as she took the envelope from my hand.

She bit her bottom lip, so quickly I almost missed it, and I almost dismissed it. But the one thing I had seen on the envelope was the sender's address: Missouri, USA.

I gave Niinu her jacket and she promised she would arrange the coffee, leaving me with the guests and a list of interviews to be resumed after the break.

As soon as Niinu was gone, I walked to the

dining room, pausing with my hand on the door, cursing my initial enthusiasm as I began to wonder what I had gotten myself into.

Part 13

Everyone spoke at once. Between accusations and insinuations including Hogan's obsession with his watch, Jordan's useless dietary advice, and the suspicious motives surrounding Bradley following *the detective* to the cellar, I took another long and lingering look at the table for two tucked into the alcove of the dining room window. Between flurries of driving snow and the drifts pluming up over the rocks and onto the plates of sea ice jostling between the small fishing cutters in the harbour, there was a sense of calm, so far removed from the storm that raged between the hotel guests. They quietened down as Niinu arrived with a trolley of fresh coffee and a small selection of cakes. Jordan apologised for their behaviour, while Hogan helped himself to more cakes and sugar in his coffee than I imagined a dentist would recommend. But as the heat of their argument settled into a warm exchange of pleasantries about the smell of the coffee and the number of blueberries in the slices of cake, I realised they were waiting for me to say something, so I told them about the coffins.

"In the basement?" Georgina asked.

"Yes," I said, pausing as Niinu dropped a cup onto the floor. She apologised, catching my eye, if only briefly, before excusing herself and hurrying back to the kitchen.

"How many?" Claudia asked.

"Three that I could see," I said. I waited until they were seated before telling them what I knew of coffins in Greenland. It wasn't a lot, but it made a little more sense when I explained that the coffins were old and unused. I didn't mention the paint.

"And you say that carpenters stored the coffins under their houses?" Jordan said.

"Yes." I sat down as Georgina gestured at the chair next to her. "You can't dig graves in the winter," I said.

"Permafrost," Hogan said. "I read about it."

I nodded once, and then again as Jordan offered to pour me a cup of coffee. "So," I said, as she placed the coffee on the table in front of me. "Years ago, the bodies would be kept in the coffins under the carpenter's house, until the ground thawed in the summer and they could be buried."

"Like a mortuary, honey?" Jordan asked.

"More like a chapel," I said.

"Claudia's a carpenter," Hogan said, turning to look at her. "Got any bodies in your basement, Claudia?"

"No," she said. "But you just say the word, and I'll build you a coffin."

"Really?" Hogan snorted. "I bet you'd like that."

"I would," she said. "But only if you've got insurance."

"That's enough, you two," Jordan said. "The detective is just trying to help."

"I'm just a constable," I said, but my words

were lost in another round of squabbling until Mosaic raised his voice, slapping his hand on the table to be heard.

"Hey. People," he said. "Just stop, already. I want to know what Bradley said down in the cellar."

"What he said?" Hogan snorted for a second time. "It doesn't matter what he *said*. It's the fact that he followed the detective down there at all that interests me. I mean, did anyone else know there was a basement?"

"Actually," I said. "It's more like a wall of wood around the rocks."

"Whatever," Hogan said. "I didn't know there was a basement."

"Bradley builds condos," Claudia said. "Of course, he knew there would be a basement. And then he saw her," she said, pointing a thick finger at me. "So he followed her."

"Why?" Mosaic said. "There's a storm. What made him want to follow her so bad he'd go out in a storm? I mean, is he trying to hide something?"

"We don't know that," Jordan said. "And now he's in hospital."

"Right," Mosaic said. "He's the victim now, playing his part." He waved his long cuffs at Hogan as he started to speak, shushing the others with a scowl before he continued. "Does anyone else remember the call Bradley got at dinner? The one from the IRS? He's under investigation. Probably fraud. They found him out."

"Fraud?" I said.

"That's right, *detective*." Mosaic pushed back

from the table and stood up. He made a show of walking to the coffee trolley, drawing out his story as he poured another cup for himself, before generously offering to top up everyone else's, milking the limelight. "Think about it. Those condos that burned down. Remember? Was it coincidence that Justin insured them? I don't think so. And then Justin goes missing. It was Bradley who offered to clean out Justin's office. But I bet none of you ever asked what he was looking for. Did you?"

"What do you mean?" Jordan said. "What was he looking for?"

"Receipts, chits, evidence," Mosaic said, as he walked back to his seat.

I could see it now, the missing link drawing them all together. Each of them knew Justin as an insurance broker first, and a friend – perhaps even a distant friend – second. He connected them.

Hogan cut through a moment of awkward silence with a long, hearty laugh, spilling cake crumbs from his mouth and drawing disgusted looks from Jordan and Georgina. Claudia turned away from him, catching my eye for a moment with what felt like a penetrating stare, as if she was trying to figure out what I knew, or what I might deduce from the talk around the table. She excused herself a second later, grabbing her jacket from the back of her chair and walking across the room.

"Don't forget to talk to the detective," Jordan called out, as Claudia reached the door.

"Whenever she's ready," Claudia said over her shoulder.

My phone rang as she left the dining room, and I retreated to a quiet corner to answer it, smiling at the name of the caller displayed on the screen.

"Hey, Atii," I said, as I answered her call.

"Where are you?"

"Uummannaq."

"Still?"

"I'm stranded, Atii. Stuck here until the storm blows over."

"You poor thing, P. Trapped on an island. What are you doing?"

I paused to look around the room, catching fragments of more arguments, this time about insurance, and who had insured what and for how much.

"I'm working on a missing persons case. I think."

"You think?"

"Yes," I said. "But right now, I'm wondering if it was murder."

Part 14

There are very few murders in Greenland. The majority of violent situations in Greenland usually involved people who knew each other, but rarely did they end in murder. While some of the victims were seriously hurt, there was often something linking them to the person or persons hurting them. In small communities, such violent episodes could sometimes be prevented as the local police and community workers coordinated their efforts to support the families, and to keep an eye on them, especially those families with children. In Tikaajaat's case, they sent him to Nuuk. But even in a country with a gun in almost every house, murder was a rare event.

I finished my call with Atii, promising to stay safe and to keep her updated. I pictured her at home, watching another episode of *Friends*, or something similar, relaxing before her next shift. I thought about the hard bed back in my hotel room and felt a sudden pang of longing for my own bed, my own apartment. I spared an evil thought for Sergeant Duneq, wondering if he had seen the *Suluk* article online, followed by another evil thought that I could leave a copy of the in-flight magazine in his pigeon hole when I got back to Nuuk. He assigned me to prisoner escort to get me out of the city, to keep me away from the missing persons desk. And now, thanks to his scheming, I was working a missing persons case. But where it might lead, was anyone's guess. I needed to collect my thoughts.

I slipped out of the dining room and into the hotel reception. Juuliu's power screwdriver was back on Niinu's desk, and two batteries were plugged in and charging. I paused to listen for the door banging in the wind, nodding when I heard it. Juuliu had yet to screw the door shut, and I wondered if I should have another look in the cellar, only to realise that I still couldn't get inside the inner room, unless there was another door leading down to it, perhaps from some other room in the hotel. I tried to picture the location of the cellar, closing my eyes, and turning on the spot on the reception carpet, as I tried to orientate myself. Spatial relations wasn't one of my strong points, but if I concentrated I could picture the location of the cellar beneath me, and the inner room a little forward and to the right. I turned, opened my eyes, and looked straight at the kitchen door, pinched between the dining room to the left and the study to the right.

The kitchen had a narrow entrance, with a side door into the dining room, and a wall with the outline of a door, now filled-in, that confirmed my earlier thought that the study was once a pantry. The kitchen itself opened up into a large working area with a walk-in freezer on my left. By my own reckoning, the freezer was directly above the room in the cellar. I reached for the handle, only to jump at the sound of someone saying my name.

"It is Petra, isn't it, Honey?" Jordan asked as she stepped into the kitchen.

"Yes," I said.

I let go of the door handle, noting that the key was broken in the lock, and that there were two D rings, one on the door and one on the frame, where I might have expected to see a clasp.

"I just wondered if you were ready for me?" Jordan looked at her watch. "Only, it's getting late, and it looks like everyone wants to stay up until we're done, and, well, I just wanted to move things along a bit. If that's all right with you?"

"It's fine," I said, shelving my thoughts of what might be inside the freezer, and, more importantly, what might be below it. "Shall we sit in the study?"

"Yes," she said. "I'll follow you."

Part 15

There was something different about Jordan. Gone was the nervous ring twisting I noticed the first time she came into the study. She was stronger now, and I wondered if it had anything to do with Bradley Washington, and Mosaic's implications regarding his behaviour. The Jordan I sat next to at dinner had returned, and she smiled as I sat down opposite her.

"What do you want to know, honey?"

Not for the first time, I felt the need to remind Jordan – to remind all of them – that this was not my idea, that I wasn't a detective, and that I was just stranded on the island, waiting for a break in the weather before returning to Nuuk.

But I didn't say anything.

I was too curious to stop now.

"How about I tell you about myself? How's that, honey?"

Jordan didn't wait for me to answer. She made herself comfortable in the chair, crossing her long legs before she began. I tried to guess her age as she talked, noting the fine wrinkles around her mouth and the tightness of her skin. I thought she was in her mid to late fifties, and her story confirmed it.

"I wasn't always a dietician," she said. "I started out in entertainment. I was a dancer. You know, like a showgirl?" Jordan uncrossed her legs, lifting one of them high above the desk, making me wonder if I could do the same. "I worked all the shows in Vegas, met so many people, caught so many breaks. But I always knew it was a short-term gig. None of the girls were much older than thirty, not back then anyway. So, right before the summer, back in the 90s, I took my money, borrowed a car – a convertible – and I took a road trip. Just me, a couple hundred dollars, and a tank of gas. So liberating."

I could just see the desert roads that Jordan described, could almost feel the hot wind blowing through my hair, and I thought about Atii, how the two of us should take a road trip, before either of us settled down. America would be perfect, especially as there are no roads between the towns and villages in Greenland.

"And that's when I met Justin."

"In the 90s?" I asked. I felt the pinch of my skin between my eyes as I tried to remember how old Justin was in the photo. He didn't look much older than Niinu.

"Late nineties. Maybe 1999. He was just a kid then, honey. He could have been ten or eleven. He had these big brown eyes." The skin around Jordan's eyes creased as she smiled. "I was wearing my showgirl shorts and he couldn't take his eyes off my legs. Of course, I didn't mind. I was used to people looking. It was my job. Anyway," Jordan said with a sigh. "Justin's father was the real catch. He sold insurance and I told him he could try and sell me insurance if he bought me dinner." Jordan paused at the memory. "That was the funniest thing.

Little Justin spent the whole night staring at me, right up until the time his daddy started talking insurance. Then he switched from me to his dad, as if there was nothing more interesting than talking premiums and percentages. I remember," she said, with another smile, "he took one of his daddy's pens – plucked it right out of his shirt pocket – then started writing figures on a napkin. Even back then, he had a head for figures. Put that together with his looks and as soon he could he started selling insurance. He never went to college."

"Did he sell you insurance?"

"Justin or his daddy?" Jordan laughed. "His daddy didn't sell me anything. I let him pay for my dinner, and I even think he bought me a full tank of gas, but he didn't sell me any insurance."

"But Justin did."

"He sure did, honey. Many years later. You see, his daddy and I swapped addresses; we kept in touch. And that's another funny thing. Justin didn't just have a head for numbers, he had a way about him. I called it his *disaster anticipation*, or something like that. It was like he could predict the most obscure little disasters, then write an insurance policy for that very thing, with the highest rewards at the lowest rates. Then, when the unthinkable happened, we all cashed in."

"Cashed in?"

"I'm sorry, honey. Is it my English? Am I talking too fast?"

"No," I said. "I'm just curious."

"About our insurances? Hell, *everybody's* curious about Justin's insurances. He had to change his company name a few times. He changed the location too." Jordan paused, as if suddenly remembering she was talking to a police officer. "This is a casual talk, detective, isn't it?"

"I'm only a constable," I said.

"That's right. Of course you are. Silly me, I was just thinking about extradition. Like if I told you something here would you be compelled to do something about it?"

"As long as you haven't committed a crime in Greenland," I said. I slipped my hand into my pocket, wondering how Jordan would react if I put my smartphone on the desk. I decided I would just have to make notes once we were finished.

"Crime is such a rotten word," she said. "I don't think what Justin did was *criminal*, although, maybe you should ask Bradley about that, honey. He's the one getting calls from the IRS."

"IRS?"

"Inland Revenue Service. They've been investigating him on and off ever since the fire. Somehow his condos burned down."

"Was it arson?"

"Lightning," Jordan said. "The strangest thing. It was like the finger of God reaching down, touching Bradley's condos on the very day they were finished, and then torching them. All three."

"We don't have lighting in Greenland," I said.

"Never?"

"Maybe once a year, around Nuuk. Sometimes never." I shrugged. "It's the climate. Too dry, I think."

"That's curious."

"Yes," I said. "But Bradley's condos... Did the lightning strike one of them and the fire spread to the others?"

"Oh no, honey. All three of the condos got hit by lighting."

"But lightning strikes are part of a normal insurance. Aren't they?"

"That's right. But Justin wrote an extra clause in the event that all three condos were struck by lightning on the same day. I think they call it *force majeure*, when something extraordinary happens. But lightning isn't extraordinary, so writing a special clause for three strikes on the same day, didn't raise too many eyebrows. He got away with it."

"But if they were all in the same place," I said, as the pinch of skin between my eyes tightened.

"Oh no, honey, Bradley was building condos in three different locations. Lightning was always a possibility, but Justin made it more interesting with the *all in one day* clause. Of course, *that's* what the IRS are so keen to investigate. It raised their eyebrows. That and when they caught him going through Justin's office after his disappearance."

"Bradley was in Justin's office?"

"Back in Lincoln, Missouri, honey. He said he was just helping out and cleaning up, once Justin was legally declared dead. He took Justin's computer, his extra hard drives and all the paper he could find. Justin's dad was dead – car accident. His mother was nowhere to be found, and Bradley was just doing what any friend would do. That's what he said. But you have to wonder what he was looking for."

I nodded, but a lot of what Jordan said passed over my head, as I focused on one word, the location of Justin's office in *Missouri*.

Part 16

Just as Jordan and I were finishing up, Georgina brought Claudia to the study, and I caught a whisper of something that sounded like a reminder, that they had all agreed to do it, and that Claudia should cooperate, if she was capable of that. The three women bunched at the door, as Jordan left, stepping to one side to give Claudia room to enter. I caught Georgina's eye as she waited at the door, but she was focused on Claudia, and as soon as Claudia started to speak, I understood why.

"She told you about the lightning?" she said, hiking a large thumb over her shoulder as Georgina and Jordan retreated to the dining room.

"Yes," I said, as I switched on the recording app on my phone. "Is it okay if I record the interview?"

"Interview?" Claudia shrugged. "Whatever. I've got nothing to hide."

I paused when she said that, curious that people rarely said it unless there *was* something to hide. It didn't mean that they were hiding something big, but often it was enough to make the statement a lie, however small. Claudia stared at me, and I suddenly felt naked without my utility belt, folding nightstick, and pistol. The desk between us was sturdy, but Claudia and I were the same height, and

I didn't doubt that she could easily reach across it. While Hogan might be the loudest of the group, and Bradley the biggest, Claudia was the most intimidating, and I began to appreciate why Jordan was quick to step out of her way, and why Georgina might have apprehensions about leaving Claudia alone with me in the study. I decided on a gentle course of questioning and picked up where Claudia had left off.

"Tell me about the lightning," I said.

"What about it?"

"You mentioned it."

"So?"

"You wanted to know if Jordan had said anything about it."

"Did she?"

I bit my lip as I realised the roles had been reversed, that it was Claudia asking the questions, and I was feeding her short answers in an attempt to get her to talk.

"You're not very good at this, are you?" she said, cracking her knuckles as she waited for me to respond. "But then, you've been trying to tell us all night, you're just a…"

"Constable," I said.

"Not a detective."

"No."

"All right, *Constable*," Claudia said. "Now we've got that cleared up. What do we do next?"

"Do?"

"This is still an interview, right?"

"Yes," I said, although, up to that point, it was one of the more difficult interviews of my career.

"If I'm going to help you find out what happened to Justin…"

"Another one of Hogan's stupid ideas," Claudia said.

"You don't want my help?"

"I didn't say that." Claudia glanced over her shoulder, as if she half-expected someone to be watching and listening. "I promised Georgina I would be helpful. That I wouldn't be so combative."

"Are you?"

"What?"

"Combative?"

She certainly looked *combative*, but there was something else, just a little deeper. I could see it in her eyes. If Tuukula had been there he would have noticed it. He might even have whispered in my ear, or, more likely, asked a cryptic question with a raised eyebrow, while he waited for me to figure it out for myself. I suddenly felt incredibly alone, and vulnerable, and longed for a more familiar face. I started at what felt like phantom palms on my thighs, as if Luui was squirming into my lap, making herself comfortable. It was at once alarming and reassuring, and the presence – whether a figment of my own imagination or a shamanic projection – was enough to give me a boost of confidence.

"What just happened?" Claudia asked.

"When?"

"Just now." She raised a stubby finger and let it drift between us, pointing at my eyes, before letting her hand fall to her thigh. "It's like you were gone for a moment."

"Maybe I was," I said. "It's been a long day."

"And it's getting late."

I let my shoulders sag a little, and then thought once more about Tikaajaat, and how chatty he had been on the flight from Kulusuk to Nuuk. A little caffeine and a few kind words had really opened him up. Claudia, regardless of the tough image she projected, looked like someone who could really use a chat, a chance to talk.

I reached for my smartphone, turned the recording app off, and slipped it into my pocket.

"What are you doing?" she said with a frown creasing her wide forehead.

I stood up, mentally brushing Luui from my lap and sent a silent *thanks* northwards. I gestured at the door, and said, "I'd like a coffee. I think there might be some left in the kitchen."

I didn't wait for Claudia. I just smiled as I walked around the desk and out of the study. I heard the creak of her chair as she stood up and then the heavy tread of her boots as she followed me to the kitchen.

"There's no fresh milk," I said, as I plucked two clean cups from the coffee trolley. "But the UHT milk isn't so bad if it's cold."

"I'll take it straight, no cream," Claudia said, nodding her thanks as I handed her a cup. "I don't know how you cope with life up here." Claudia leaned against the kitchen counter, and I rested against the oven in the centre of the kitchen, sipping my coffee as she talked. "I mean, it's so barren, so cold, and the milk…"

"We get fresh milk in Nuuk," I said.

"How?"

"On a ship from Denmark."

"And how about the cold? Is it always like this?"

I paused for a second to listen for the storm. The wind had died down a little, reducing the bang and thud of the cellar door to a softer slap and crack.

"There are storms in the fall and spring. Then, in summer, if we've had a few days of clear skies with lots of sun, we'll have a day or two of wind." I shrugged. "It's just the way it is."

"But it doesn't rain?"

"In Nuuk? It rains a lot, half the year – at least, that's what it feels like. But up here. I don't know. It's drier, I guess."

"You're not from the island?"

"I grew up in Nuuk," I said. "I'm a city girl."

"I grew up on a farm." Claudia put her cup down and held up her hands. "See? Farmer's hands. As a kid, I learned how to fork hay and wring chicken necks before I started school. And when I got to school, if there was a fight, you can bet I was in it. It got so bad, even when I wasn't fighting, they had my parents come pick me up. I think it made the other parents feel safer."

"You had a temper," I said, recalling a few of my own fights in the schoolyard, and at the Children's Home.

"Still do." Claudia cast a glance at the door, and then said, "You've seen the way they look at me. Like they're scared."

"Why?"

"Why are they scared?" Claudia reached for her cup and poured herself another coffee. There was something new in her eyes when she turned around – a sharp light, burning with a new intensity. "They all told you stuff. I bet they told you about Justin and his insurance scams."

"Scams?"

"Yeah, you know, a *fraud*. Because that's what he was – a real fraud. Sure, he was nice guy, and he was real nice to me. We met in high school. Not many guys had paid me much attention, but Justin was different. He was soft when he wanted to be, when he wasn't distracted."

Claudia looked at the door leading to reception, and I wondered who she expected to walk through it.

"So, I fell for him. He was a bit older, and I just worshipped the ground he walked on. And he knew that. Even I could see that. But I didn't care. And then, later, when he asked me to help him out, I was ready to do anything. I didn't even care about the money, even though he said there would be a lot of it, once things started to pan out."

I had to concentrate as Claudia relaxed into her story, as the words flowed into a softer southern accent. I used to think I was good at English, but some of the words escaped me, until Claudia said something that reminded me of what Jordan had said earlier.

"Jordan said something about *disaster anticipation*," I said.

"She said that?" Claudia laughed.

"She said he was good at it."

"There was nothing to anticipate," Claudia said. "There was nothing magic about those disasters. Justin either knew they were going to happen, or he made sure they happened."

"Like the lightning," I said.

"Yeah, like lightning. I mean, how about that? Sure, lightning can strike more than a few places during a storm, and that's what Justin was counting on. He just waited for a storm, then made sure lightning struck where he wanted it to."

"How did he do that?"

A wry smile curled the corner of Claudia's mouth. "He just asked. That's how."

I listened as Claudia explained how Justin convinced Bradley to hire her to work on his condos, and how she had helped the electrician with the wiring.

"I even did a little myself, when the electrician called in sick one day."

"And the lightning?"

"There was a storm, and there were a couple of strikes. And then a couple more, if you know what I mean?"

I think I did, but Claudia's insight into Justin's ability to anticipate disaster left me wondering.

"Did he ask you to help with other things too?"

"Other scams, you mean?"

"Yes," I said, curious as to how far Claudia was willing to go, how much she was prepared to tell me.

"I liked Justin," she said. "I liked him a lot. He made me feel safe. He made me feel wanted."

"So, when he asked?"

"I said *yes*." Claudia shifted on her feet, pressing a thick thumb to her eye, and catching a tear in the whorls of her skin. "Of course, you could never prove it," she said, sniffing back another tear before looking at me. "At least not directly. All the policies were on file – on his computer and in some banker boxes in the office."

"In Missouri," I said.

"Right."

Claudia paused, as if waiting for me to reveal what I knew about Missouri.

"Jordan said Bradley helped clean out the office."

"Oh yeah. That's *exactly* what he did."

I felt a breath of cold air on my cheek, as if Tuukula was standing beside me. The bigger picture was forming, and I could see it now. Justin with his uncanny ability to write the most unlikely policies with the lowest premiums, and the greatest benefits. Claudia made them happen, allowing everyone else in the group to reap the rewards. But only if someone tidied everything up, sweeping away the trail. Someone like Bradley.

"But," I said, feeling the pinch of my skin above my nose. "Justin was a broker. What about the companies that underwrite the policies? They would have records."

"Justin had a way around that. He worked with insurance companies who were connected to hedge funds – people with more money than sense, sometimes. He rarely used the same company twice and would always have this *what are the odds* kind of smile ready whenever they questioned him about it, right up to the moment they had to pay up."

"And then?"

"He handled the money, took his cut, and then changed his company name."

"What was his cut?"

"He took thirteen percent, sometimes fifteen."

"Is that a lot?"

"Most brokers take two to eight percent on the premiums. But Justin took his cut of the compensation. Thirteen percent of three condos is a lot of money," she said.

"Yes," I said, as another cold breath tickled my cheek.

It was beginning to make sense, how such an unlikely group of people came together. But the bigger question of why they might stay together, especially after Justin's disappearance, still remained unsolved, and I felt the pinch of my frown deepen.

Part 17

I was still reluctant to disturb Simonsen's evening off. Nor did I want to bring in the officer on duty. Until such time as I had hard evidence that a crime had been committed, I was, technically, just an off-duty constable talking with tourists about a missing persons case, that, according to Niinu, was closed nearly two years ago. Simonsen hadn't found Justin Moon's body then, and I had nothing new to add to the case. Justin was going to remain *disappeared* long after the weather cleared, and long after everyone went home.

And yet, two years after his disappearance, his friends and acquaintances came back.

Why?

I tidied away the milk and coffee, lingering by the freezer, if only to look at the handle one more time, before putting the carton of milk in the refrigerator. The location of the walk-in freezer still fit with where I had positioned the inner cellar in my mind, and I was tempted to look inside.

The door opened easily, almost *too* easily, as if it had been broken once, and the seal had never quite been the same. There were shelves lining the three walls, and cardboard boxes of imported vegetables on a table in the middle of the freezer. I wondered what tourists would make of the freezer as it also stored a range of deep-frozen Greenlandic delicacies in various states of preparation. Sea gulls hung upside down like lazy white bats, with hooks tucked beneath string tied around their feet. They had not been plucked. Arctic hare hung beside them, in much the same way. Seal ribs were also hooked and hanging from a rack stretching the width of the freezer room, together with huge slabs of liver-dark meat, which I recognised as fin whale. To the outsider it was undoubtedly a macabre collection of Arctic birds and mammals, but to a local, it was a rich collection of energy-giving meats, apart from the gulls. I had yet to meet anyone who ever really craved a breast of what was often referred to as Greenlandic chicken.

But I wasn't looking for meat and vegetables.

I walked around the table, squeezing between one side and the shelves, knocking the seal ribs, and throwing shadows on the walls as the ribs swayed in front of the naked yellow bulb. The door closed with a soft snick, but I didn't think anything of it, as closer inspection of a tear in the linoleum covering the floor revealed a rectangular piece that could, if I moved the table, be removed. I lifted a corner, holding my breath as I pulled the linoleum flap past a handle cut into a recess of what looked like a trap door.

"Leading down into the cellar," I said. My breath frosted in front of my face, coating the tips of my black hair in brittle white sleeves of ice.

I let the flap fall back onto the floor and walked around the table to the door. I needed help to move the table if I was going to get access to the cellar.

I gripped the door handle, letting go as I felt the metal stick to my warm palms. I tried again, using the sleeve of my shirt as a glove. The handle turned but the door didn't budge. The seal was better than I had thought, and now, despite my Greenlandic genes, the cold was beginning to affect me, and not just with thicker sleeves of ice in my hair, but with a stiffening of the fine hairs on my arms, ice coating my eyelashes, and a tightening of my skin.

I was stuck inside the freezer.

I gave up on the door and tried my phone, cursing the lack of signal, before chiding myself for even thinking that I would be able to get one. The walls of the freezer room were metal, everything was insulated, and, in a horrible moment, I wondered if it would be soundproofed too.

Still clutching my phone in one hand, I bunched my hands into fists and drummed the door, yelling for help. The thumps and echoes rippled around the walls, and the vibration set more ribs twisting in the light. The dead gulls spun from their hooked feet, beaks clacking against cold metal each time they hit the wall. The hares thumped their frozen flanks against each other, and, as I misted the chill air with breathy shouts, the bulb dulled with puckered patterns of ice.

I stopped banging, forcing myself to stay calm, and take several deep, cold breaths, as I considered my options and planned my next move.

It was still cold outside the hotel, but no colder than the inside of the freezer. It might even be warmer below the freezer. I looked at the table, clenching my jaw as my teeth started to clatter. If I had found help, I would have stacked the boxes to one side, then moved the table out of the freezer and into the kitchen.

But I didn't have help. Nor did I have my jacket, or even my utility belt. I had no tools. Only a useless smartphone, and a pair of regulation boots.

"Training is over, Jensen."

Of course, of all the voices I could channel in that moment, of all the help and assistance I might want, it had to be Sergeant Duneq who spurred me into action. The thought of him shaking his head and wobbling his jowls at the news of me being found dead in a hotel freezer, together with a host of *I told you so* comments that he was so very good at, gave me the strength to brace myself against the door, and kick at the table, again and again until it rocked and then crashed onto the floor. I reached for the flap of linoleum, tearing it off the floor, only to gasp, breathless, as the trapdoor refused to budge, sealing my fate.

Part 18

I tucked a piece of cardboard under my bottom and hugged my knees to my chest. My teeth chattered until I clamped my chin between my knees, convincing myself that I wasn't giving up, I was just regrouping, or *rethinking*. I was doing *something*, or rather I thought I had better *start* doing something, as freezing to death in a walk-in freezer just wasn't how I wanted my life to end. Once the thought was out there, it felt logical to explore the alternatives. Death was always close at hand in Greenland. Of course, there were plenty of ways to die in other countries, but the difference in Greenland was that just hurting oneself could mean death when help was often so very far away. The weather played its part too, helping or hindering the help in ever reaching the victim.

Victim.

That's what I was or was in danger of becoming.

Being a victim should have come naturally to me. I lost my parents before I could remember. I grew up with strangers in a Children's Home. I never learned the language of my country and struggled with my identity because of it. I had every chance to *be* the victim, but somehow, I had always resisted it. Somehow, I had fought back. And I damned well wasn't going to give up twenty-three years of fighting to be me, just to die in a hotel freezer.

I pushed myself to my feet, clamped my jaw shut, and strode to the door.

The first few thumps with my fists were pathetic, as the base of my palm was too soft to make much more than a soft thud that echoed inside the freezer rather than out into the kitchen. I tried punching instead, yelling with each crunch of my knuckles, slamming them harder and harder, screaming away the pain and the cold, oblivious of what, if anything was happening outside the freezer, until, finally, I heard someone shouting for me to stop from the other side of the door.

"You have to stop. The door is locked. I'm trying to open it."

I stopped, letting my fists fall to my sides, ignoring the throbbing in my knuckles as I wondered how the door could be locked. There was no lock. The key had been broken off inside it, and the clasp ripped away, leaving just two metal rings with nothing to connect them.

"Petra," Niinu said, as she opened the door.

I stepped into the kitchen, feeling the warm, dry air wash over me, as Niinu pulled me into her arms. I shivered in her grip, until we sank to the floor and I pressed my arms around her, partly for warmth, drawing her heat into my body, but also to stop the shaking – mine *and* hers.

"He promised it would never happen again," Niinu said.

I heard the words but struggled to say anything.

I was too cold, and my throat stung from shouting and screaming.

"He promised."

I stopped shaking long before Niinu did. When I felt her hot tears running down my neck, I managed to lift my head and find my voice.

"Who promised?" I said, after clearing my throat.

"*Ataata*," she said. "He was supposed to fix it, so it could never happen again."

"Fix what?"

"The door." Niinu lifted her head, and I felt her hands slide off my back as she relaxed her grip. "He broke the key in the lock. He removed the clasp. But still," she said, showing me the tongs, she held in her hand. "Still it could be locked."

"It was locked?"

"*Aap*. Someone stuffed these into the rings."

I took the slim tongs from Niinu's hand, stifling a laugh as I realised I might have died because of a kitchen utensil.

"For olives," Niinu said. "When we have a salad bar."

"Someone locked me in the freezer," I said, clenching my bloody fist around the tongs.

"*Aap*."

"And its happened before?"

Niinu looked into my eyes for a moment, then dipped her head, turning away. I wanted to ask her about it but struggled to think further than the fact that someone had deliberately shut me inside the freezer. The list of suspects was short. But I wanted to finish the interviews before I confronted any of them.

"Niinu," I said. "Let's pretend this didn't happen."

"What?"

"I don't want you to say anything."

"Why?"

"Because now I want to finish this. I want to find out what happened to Justin, but it's personal now." I pressed the tongs into Niinu's hand, and then reached up to the counter to pull myself onto my feet. "But I'll need your help," I said. "And one more thing."

Niinu waited as I brushed the last of the frost from my hair.

"I'd like to borrow your fleece."

Niinu stood up and removed her jacket. She watched as I pulled it on and zipped it to my chin. The shivering had slowed and I felt almost warm again. I patted the pockets to make sure there wasn't anything inside them. The last thing I wanted to do was crumple another of Niinu's personal letters. That's when I remembered *Missouri*.

"I'm sorry, Niinu," I said. "But there is one more thing you can help me with."

Niinu raised her eyebrows, the silent Greenlandic *yes*.

"I'm going to talk to Georgina. But I'd like to talk to you afterwards. Before you go home."

Niinu nodded and excused herself. I waited as she walked out of the kitchen, and then checked my phone. It was time to call Simonsen.

Part 19

Uummannaq's chief of police held a grand title with plenty of responsibility concentrated in a small population spread out over seven settlements, with varying degrees of accessibility. To disturb him on a night off was, as I discovered, like goading dragons, or at least, that's what it felt like. The fact that it was late, and the storm was still raging, only added to Simonsen's abrasive manner as he responded to my call for help. We agreed that he would come to the hotel in one hour.

"Just don't do anything stupid, Constable," he said.

"I'll try not to."

Simonsen's concern was carefully wrapped inside a mouthful of grit, but it made me smile – my first since Niinu rescued me from the freezer.

I picked up my phone charger from my room before I went looking for Georgina, setting it to charge and placing it on the desk between us as I started the interview.

"Are you all right?" she asked. "You look a bit peaky?"

I nodded that I was fine, but my cheeks were flushed and probably quite rosy. I said nothing about the freezer, preferring to keep the incident quiet until Simonsen arrived.

"What do you want to know, Detective?"

I was too tired to correct her and jumped right in with a more direct line of questioning than I had taken with her travelling companions – I no longer thought of them as friends.

"What happened the night Justin disappeared?"

"You mean the very night?"

"Yes."

"It's such a long time ago," Georgina said. "I'm not sure I can remember all the details."

I checked that the app on my smartphone was recording, and then leaned back in my chair as Georgina recalled the last night of her previous visit to Greenland.

"We ate together," she said. "We all sat at the same table. Of course, Claudia sat next to Justin, again. She was besotted with him; we all knew it. But Justin had eyes for someone else that night." Georgina's lips creased at the memory, and I was tempted to ask who, but she continued before I could say anything. "Then we agreed to have a Greenlandic coffee. You know, the one with all the spirits and liqueurs to represent the land, and the sea, and the…"

My thoughts drifted as she described the drink invented for tourists. I had never enjoyed it, and could rarely justify the cost of it, but the tourists seem to get a kick out of it. Instead, I wondered who might have caught Justin's attention, and I realised I had known ever since I found Niinu's letter in her jacket pocket.

"And then I saw Justin leave the hotel, to go for a walk."

"Sorry," I said, as I jolted back into Georgina's recollection of the events leading up to Justin's disappearance. "He went for a walk?"

"Yes."

"But there was a storm," I said. "Everyone agrees on that."

"It was pretty wild," Georgina said. "But I guess Justin wanted to feel the power of nature, if you know what I mean? He could be like that at times. It was part of his charm."

A shadow of something flickered across Georgina's eyes, and I wondered just how fond her recollections of Justin were.

"And did you see him return?"

"You mean did I see him come back to the hotel? No," she said. "I never saw him again." Georgina shifted in her seat, scratching at a stain she noticed on her trousers. It felt like a diversion, as if she was considering what to say next. She tutted at the stain, then clasped her hands in her lap, lifting her head to look at me. "I don't know what Claudia told you," she said. "But perhaps you could ask her where she was that evening. Everyone knew she had a crush on Justin. And he just played her along. She would do anything for him. *Anything.* If that isn't enough to make one wonder, then I don't know what is."

"Wonder about what?"

"Her motives, of course."

Georgina tilted her head slightly to one side, as if she was dealing with a small child. She was different to how she had been on the plane when I first met her, and even at dinner. Something had changed, and it made me wonder if she knew anything about the freezer, and how I came to be locked inside it.

"You think Claudia did something to Justin?"

"I think she had every reason to. Especially after he was so taken with the young Greenlander in reception."

"Niinu?"

Georgina nodded. "It wasn't the first time they had met. They knew each other from Justin's previous visits to Greenland. He had an adventurous streak, something he applied to his business, and in his free time. Of course, with all the money he was making, he could afford to come to places like Greenland. And, obviously, he liked it here. So much so he persuaded us to come with him. He called it *a trip of a lifetime*, because, as you know, it's so expensive to come here."

"And you all decided to come on this trip together?"

"Yes."

"As friends?"

Georgina nibbled at her lip as she thought, and then said, "You think we're friends?"

"No," I said.

"But you called us *friends*."

"I think you're connected," I said. "I think Justin connects you."

"Of course, he does. We're all in his pocket, even now."

"Because of the insurances?"

"Yes." Georgina sneered as she spat the word from her mouth. "Those damned things, and that bloody man." She shifted in her seat, fidgeting with an energy that seemed to come from somewhere deep inside her. "You know, he insured anything for anyone."

"I know he insured the fur on your dog," I said.

"Hogan told you that, did he?"

"Yes."

Georgina's cheeks flushed with a heat to match the fire burning in her eyes.

"He probably told you that Portland shed his fur, that he had a disease. It wasn't the mange, if that's what you're thinking. It was hereditary, something the breeder should have told me. The compensation I got for handfuls of fur, was nothing to what I could have got for the chance to put Portland out to stud. His pedigree was impeccable, or it should have been, if she hadn't conned me. I would have been better off with the other insurance Justin wrote."

"For Portland?" I asked, my brow pinching as I tried to keep up.

"What?"

"You said something about another insurance?"

"Did I?" Georgina said. She turned her attention back to the stain on her trousers, then stood up suddenly, flicking her finger at my smartphone. "You have everything you need, Detective. I saw Justin leave. No one saw him come back. He probably shivered to death on his walk, or maybe fell through the ice. It would be just like Justin to stride out onto the sea ice in a storm. Or maybe someone pushed him?" Georgina shrugged. "But what do I know? I wasn't in love with him."

She turned, and walked to the door, stopping briefly with one last comment.

"You're right about one thing," she said. "We're not friends. We're just forced to be with one another."

"Because of Justin."

"That's right."

"And now? You're still forced to be with each other?"

"Because Bradley didn't do his job properly. If he had, we wouldn't be here chasing ghosts."

She left before I could ask another question, brushing past Niinu, as she hovered by the door.

"I'm going home soon," Niinu said. "But I'm ready to talk now. If you want to hear what I have to say?"

"Yes," I said. "But not here. Is there somewhere else we could go?"

Niinu nodded, and then pointed back towards reception. "We can go to the office," she said. "It's quieter there."

Part 20

Niinu opened the office door and pointed at the tiny sofa pressed against the wall opposite the desk. She pulled a bundle of envelopes out of a drawer and placed them on the desk, before pulling one more out of the back pocket of her jeans. The envelopes were all the same size, with the same handwritten addresses. I guessed that, on closer inspection, the return address would be Lincoln, Missouri.

"From Justin to Justin," Niinu said, pressing the envelope in her hand to her nose. "This one was to me," she said, after a short sniff of the envelope.

"He wrote to you?"

"After his very first visit." Niinu looked at the empty chair by the desk, then chose to sit on the floor, curling her knees to her chest, and clutching the envelope in her hand as she rocked, gently, back and forth as she began her story. "He came on one of the adventure cruise ships one summer. I was selling beads and *Tupilaq* at a store on the grass by the harbour. Justin bought a few things, then came back to buy some more. He wasn't your typical tourist; he was too young. Most of them are old, with money. So, he was different, and exciting." She laughed and a light sparked in her eyes. "He wore one of those life vests – the tube kind that inflate if you fall in the water. The cruise ships make people wear them, even on land. Justin took his off and gave it to one of the passengers. I got worried when the tourists headed back to the boat. The ship's horn blew, and he just stayed there, chatting with me, as his ship sailed away."

"He missed his boat," I said.

"*Aap*," Niinu said. "He missed it for me." The light in her eyes shone brighter as the first tears began to slip down her cheeks. "He said I was more fun than a boat full of old people. I said he was crazy, and he said we could be crazy together." Niinu wiped her cheeks with her hand, pausing to dry a stray tear that landed on the envelope. "He stayed for two weeks, sometimes at the hotel, and then at my house, when *ataata* went fishing. He never promised anything, but he said he would be back. He came back twice, before the third and last time."

Niinu dipped her head to her knees and I got up from the sofa to join her on the floor.

"Tell me what happened," I said, softly, as I wrapped my arm around her shoulders.

"He said they were his business partners," she said, lifting her head and sniffing back another round of tears. "He didn't call them friends. He said they made money together. And he always seemed to have money, I just never thought to ask where it came from." She paused to look at the bundle of envelopes on the desk. "He started sending them a few times a year after we met. He asked me if I would hold onto them. He said they had something to do with insurance, and that was his business. But I got confused when he said they were *insurance*.

He said it was important that I keep them safe. My English is good but it's difficult when the words have two different meanings."

I knew exactly what she meant, and told her so, brushing another tear from her cheek with my thumb. "Keep going," I said, hoping that she would.

Niinu took a breath and nodded. "When I found you in the freezer, I got so scared. I knew I had to tell you. But we've told no one. Not even the police." Niinu paused for another breath, the hollow kind that are breathy with no benefits. "Justin never left Uummannaq," she said. "He's still here."

"Here?"

"In the hotel," she said, and then, "*Ataata* said he would fix the freezer door. He said it would never happen again. He broke the key in the lock. He removed the clasp. After what happened; he had to do it."

"Juuliu helped you?"

"*Aap*," Niinu said. "But he said we couldn't tell anyone. And I didn't. But then seeing you in the freezer, knowing that you might have died if I didn't find you." Niinu turned within my arms to take my hand, pressing Justin's letter between us. "The people who came with him, wanted to be with him all the time. If they saw him talking to one of the group the others joined them, as if they didn't want him to be alone with anyone. As if they didn't trust him. So, when they were here, we couldn't be together, and I wanted to be with him, like we had been the other times. But they were always there. They never let us be alone."

"So, you made a plan to meet him?" I said,

thinking it was what I would have done, before reminding myself that, probably, Atii would have made the plan and I would have done what she told me to.

"*Aap*," Niinu said. "He told them he was going for a walk. But there was a storm. And no one wanted to go outside. It was too cold. But one of them waited in the armchair in reception."

"Who?"

"Jordan, I think. It was like they were keeping an eye on him and wanted to know when he came back. I think they all agreed that she should wait."

"But he wasn't coming back that way, was he?"

"*Naamik*," Niinu said, with a shake of her head. "I told him there was another way into the hotel, that he could get back in with no one seeing him."

"How?"

"Through the cellar, and then through the trapdoor…"

"Into the freezer."

"*Aap*." Niinu gripped my hand tighter as her body started to shake. "He was supposed to come up through the trapdoor and out of the freezer, into the kitchen."

"But the door was locked," I said.

"And the key was missing." Niinu's long nails pinched my skin. "I couldn't open it and couldn't break it. I told Justin to go back down the trapdoor before he froze."

"But he couldn't."

Niinu shook her head. "The trapdoor was bolted from below." She bit her bottom lip until it turned white, and I brushed another stream of tears from her cheeks. "He was inside, and I heard him, just like I heard you, banging and kicking and shouting. I called *ataata*, but he never answered. Then I tried to get help, but there was no one around. All his friends were gone, even the woman sitting in the armchair."

"Jordan?"

"*Aap*, I think so. She was gone. The chair was empty."

"And Justin?"

I shouldn't have asked. I knew what he would have felt, as the cold seared his skin, puckered his lips, and frosted the hairs on his body, before sinking deep into his bones, slowing his body, chilling his core.

"He stopped shouting," Niinu said. "I couldn't help him."

"But your father came?" I said, after a moment's pause.

Niinu nodded, unable to speak.

I spoke for her.

"He broke into the freezer."

"*Aap*."

"But Justin was dead."

Niinu sniffed and then held her breath. She exhaled with ragged nods of her head. Then, after another pause, she found the strength to continue, her voice clearer with each step of her confession.

"*Ataata* went out of the hotel and into the cellar. He threw back the bolt and then we carried Justin through the trapdoor. There are coffins down there."

"I've seen them," I said.

"They were empty," Niinu said. "They used to

be the carpenter's but were never used. Until we put Justin inside one of them."

"You didn't tell anyone?"

"I thought I killed him." Niinu pressed her hand to her mouth, whispering through her fingers. "I *did* kill him. I told him to go outside, to sneak back into the kitchen. He died in the freezer."

"No, Niinu," I said. "It wasn't you. You didn't throw the bolt on the trapdoor. Somebody else did. Just like they locked the freezer."

"Why? Why would they do that?"

I took a moment before answering, looking once more at the envelopes on the desk, wondering if the answer was inside them.

Niinu crumpled her envelope to her face, and I teased it from her hands, flattening it on my thigh, before placing it in her lap. We both turned our heads as someone wearing heavy boots clumped along the short corridor to the office. Niinu held her breath as they knocked on the door, nodding when I asked if she was ready.

"Come in," I said, as I slid across the floor to make room for the door to open.

Simonsen looked into the room and then down at the two of us on the floor. He frowned, and then moved towards the sofa.

"Can I sit down?" he asked.

Niinu nodded, her hand still clasped to her mouth. I waited until Simonsen sat down, and then quietly closed the door.

"Niinu," I said. "I think I know what happened next. Can I tell the Chief?"

"*Aap*," she said, before hugging her knees even

tighter to her chest.

Simonsen looked at me, and I picked up the story where Niinu had stopped.

"About two years ago," I said, looking at Simonsen. "You were involved in a search for Justin Moon."

"That's right," Simonsen said, with a glance at Niinu. "We never found him."

"That's because he's in the hotel cellar…"

"What?"

"In one of the carpenter's coffins."

"What the hell?"

"Chief," I said, as Niinu started to shake. "Just listen a minute. It's not what you think."

"We searched for that man. Couldn't find him. We declared him missing, and then dead, when people said they might have seen a tourist walk out onto the ice."

"What people? Not one of the people he was travelling with?"

"Them?" Simonsen shook his head. "They all left on the first helicopter." He looked at Niinu again, and said, "He's in the cellar?"

"*Aap.*"

"In a coffin?"

"He was dead," she said.

"He froze to death," I said. "In the same way I was going to, if Niinu hadn't found me."

"Okay," Simonsen said. "One of you has to slow down, and the other has to start talking, because I have no idea what's going on right now."

Simonsen paused as the door opened and Juuliu walked into the room.

"Chief?" Juuliu said. "Is everything all right?"

"You tell me, Juuliu. It seems there's a body in your basement, and you never told me about it."

"It's okay, *ataata*," Niinu said. "I told her," she said, pointing at me. "But we have to tell the Chief."

"Tell him everything," I said, as I reached for the envelopes on the desk.

"And while they do that," Simonsen said. "Where will you be?"

"In the study, doing my last interview."

"With whom?"

"Justin Moon," I said.

Part 21

Justin was an insurance broker and his letters were his insurance. I understood that as I opened the first envelope, teasing out a folded piece of American A4 paper, slightly wider and shorter than the European equivalent. Justin had stuffed as many copies of his policies as he could into each envelope, and I spread the contents of each on the desk in front of me. The wind continued to blow, but I didn't hear it. The kitchen door creaked as someone went in and then again when they went out, but I ignored it. In front of me, in varied shades of dark grey to black ink, was a map of straight roads, bends, curves, and intersections, linking each of the people in Justin's special collection of clients. Judging from the specificity of the policies, and the degree of disaster anticipation, cleverly concealed in descriptions of the mundane, from run-of-the-mill to freak-of-nature events, the group Justin had assembled were inseparable, bound by overlapping policies, the compensation from which benefited all of them, albeit not directly, and not without some pain or misfortune.

I opened another envelope and began to see a pattern, in which one month one person benefitted, only for another to profit from that same person's misfortune in the next. What started out as relatively straightforward policies counting on the unthinkable, became calculating claims capitalising on the improbable.

I sorted the claims into piles starting with Hogan.

Hogan's wristwatch seemed to be the most practical and beneficial of the policies, saving him money each time the winder in his watch broke. But when I read the policy covering the use of faulty motors for the drills in his dental practice, the potential compensation was so good, I wondered if it was worth his while to buy better equipment.

Mosaic must have known about Hogan's dodgy drills. Why else would he have Justin write a policy that not only insured his smile, but specifically insured him against dental injury?

But Mosaic insured more than his teeth. I felt the pinch of my frown as I read and then reread his policy ensuring he was compensated in the event that his dietician ever received bad press, so bad it negatively impacted her business. Which made me wonder, how perfectly positioned Mosaic was to influence the rise or demise of his dietician, via his influential lifestyle show on *YouTube*.

Jordan seemed equally interested in bad press, with policies that insured her income against failing popularity, allowing her to explore a side interest in show dogs, Afghan Hounds in particular. But while Georgina insured herself against loss of income from Portland's hereditary mange, turning the world's most glamorous dog into a stubbly chicken – as noted in the margins of Justin's letters – Jordan insured Georgina's dogs in the event of their death.

Again, the specificity was interesting. Georgina had life insurance for her beloved Afghans, but Jordan's insurance of the same dogs covered vehicular death only.

Claudia's car was insured in the same way as Hogan's watch, with one part in particular receiving particular attention in her policy: the bumper. A quick cross-reference of the three women's claims revealed that Claudia replaced her bumper with the same frequency as Georgina's dogs died, the ones suffering from mange.

I leaned back in my chair to take a break. I could feel the pinch of my frown as I considered just how coordinated everything was, as if everybody knew everybody else's business, and policies. Why else would strangers, from different parts of the United States – spread across the whole of America, as far as I could see – have anything to do with each other. Mosaic had to know about Hogan's drills, and the three women must have known about the dogs, the bumpers, and the mange. I spared a thought for Georgina, only to purge any sympathy I might have had when I realised, she was just as calculating as everyone else. She couldn't put her dogs out to stud, if they had inferior genes.

And then there was Bradley and his condos, the ones Claudia worked on, in her capacity as amateur electrician. Judging by the letters, and the details of the policies, it seemed to be the point at which Justin's disaster anticipation faltered into the disastrous. Bradley stood to lose the most, which made it most important that his claim was successful. Justin must have convinced him it would be, and then brought Claudia in to make the improbable possible.

And that was his undoing.

Thicker envelopes with more letters revealed claims investigations, and investigations into Justin's business, and the business of all his associates. Claudia had said they were scams, but Justin's prediction of lightning striking not twice but three times in three different locations on one man's property, drew too much attention.

"And that's why he chose Greenland," I said, as another piece of the puzzle fell into place.

Not quite Europe and not quite America, Greenland was modern enough to be comfortable, but remote enough to disappear. But I don't think Justin chose to disappear permanently, just long enough to weather the storm of fraudulent claims and scams swirling around him and his associates in America.

"So, he brought them here," I said to myself, as I leaned forward to return to the letters. "To make plans to cover their tracks."

I looked up at a knock on the door, nodding as Simonsen stepped into the study.

"You were talking to yourself, Constable."

"Yes," I said.

"Find anything interesting?" Simonsen nodded at the letters spread out on the desk.

"Yes. Lots."

"And any idea who might have locked you in the freezer?"

"Yes," I said. "Some."

"All right," Simonsen said. "You can tell me in

a minute, but first we have to go down into the cellar."

Niinu pressed her jacket into my hands as I left the study. I left Justin's letters on the table, and she locked the door behind me.

"Are you all right?" I asked.

"I'm okay," she said, with a glance at Simonsen. "There are some things we have to work out."

"We'll sort it out," Simonsen said. He tugged at the collar of his jacket, then zipped it all the way above his chin. He nodded at Juuliu, as the janitor stuffed both batteries for the power screwdriver into his pockets, before leading the way into the storm. "Danielsen is on his way," Simonsen said to Niinu. "Wait for him in the office."

I reached out to hug Niinu, and then followed the Chief and Niinu's father into the last breathy gusts of the storm.

The twists and tiny tornadoes of spinning snow had settled into soft powdery plumes, dusting our boots and the cuffs of our trousers. The temperature had dropped, draining the storm's energy, dragging it down to the granite, quashing it between the exposed rocks.

The square cellar door moved listlessly, as if it too was tired of flapping. Juuliu pushed it to one side, then climbed into the cellar. I heard him slap one of the batteries into the screwdriver and begin removing the screws from one of the plywood panels, as I helped Simonsen negotiate the square door.

Once inside, Simonsen tugged the flashlight from his belt and clicked it on, just as Juuliu slid one of the panels to one side. We all blinked in the light of the yellow bulb, before following Juuliu inside the inner cellar.

"I took one of the coffins," he said, pointing at a single coffin clamped between thick granite fingers. "Do you want me to open it?"

"I think you know the answer to that," Simonsen said.

Juuliu nodded and got to work on the lid, as Simonsen turned the beam of his flashlight upwards, revealing the bolt holding the trapdoor in place. He talked as Juuliu worked on the coffin.

"Justin Moon froze to death in the freezer, and then Juuliu lowered his body down here. That's right, isn't it?" Simonsen waited for Juuliu to nod, and then continued. "So, they pulled one of the coffins up here, put Justin in it, and then sealed it off with plywood."

"Making Justin disappear," I said.

Simonsen nodded. "Right now, about the only thing I could get angry about, is the fact that they wasted police time and resources with the search. But, given the situation…"

"It was the best thing they could do."

"And Justin is listed as missing, presumed dead."

Simonsen paused as Juuliu slid the lid off the coffin. No one spoke for what felt like a minute. The chill of winter had, thankfully, purged Justin's corpse of its death smell, but the hot summer had not been kind. I took a moment more, then nodded for Juuliu to replace the lid.

"And now he's dead," Simonsen said. "Confirmed."

Part 22

We gathered in the dining room, with Justin's accomplices – now upgraded from *travelling companions* – sitting around two tables in the centre of the room, while Niinu and her father sat at the table by the window, the one I should have taken before agreeing to dining with the Americans. Simonsen leaned against the wall by the door, thumbs tucked into his utility belt in a comfortably cowboy manner. The two men sitting at the back of the room, next to the kitchen door, were strangers, although I presumed the young constable, perhaps a year or two older than me, was Danielsen. I didn't recognise the Greenlander sitting beside him.

"That's Iinta," Simonsen said, catching my arm before I addressed the group. "You're taking him back to Nuuk."

"Why is he here?"

Simonsen shrugged. "The cells are empty at the moment, and he's bored. I thought a night out would do him good. Besides, he promised to behave himself."

"Okay," I said, biting my lip for want of anything better to say.

"Are we ready, detective?" Hogan said, drumming his fingers on the table.

"*Constable*," I said, forcing a smile on my lips.

"Just like Constable Danielsen, over there, in the corner." Danielsen waved as I pointed at him. "And that's the Chief of Police, Simonsen, standing by the door."

"Chief of Police," Hogan said, and laughed. "What's the name of this place again? Amity Island?"

Simonsen laughed and said something about a film called *Jaws*, and then stepped to one side as Bradley entered the dining room. No one said a word as Bradley walked to the middle of the room. He reached out to take my hand.

"Thank you," he said. "I was out of line, and I was cold. You saved me, Constable."

"You're welcome," I said. I wanted to add that I knew exactly how he felt, but until I felt confident I knew who had slipped the tongs into the freezer door, I preferred not to say anything at all. I waited until Bradley found a seat, before reconstructing the last hours of Justin Moon's life.

All eyes were on me with the occasional glance at Niinu until I reached the part about the coffin, and the fact that Justin's body was in the hotel cellar. At that point heads began to swivel.

"You mean right this minute?" Georgina said. "He's there right now? We can see him?"

"One of you has already tried to."

"What?"

"Bradley," I said, pausing as the group turned their heads and stared at him. "When you followed me into the cellar, you said the sawdust in the snow was fresh."

"That's right."

"And Juuliu's batteries for his screwdriver were empty."

"I don't follow this," Hogan said. "You're saying one of us knew Justin was in the cellar?"

"I'm saying, someone wanted to have a look and see. The same person who knew there was a trapdoor leading into the freezer."

"Who the hell builds a hotel with a trapdoor into a freezer anyway?" Hogan said. "I mean, come on. Bradley? What do you think?"

"The hotel expanded some years ago," I said, with a nod to Juuliu. "I've already told you about the carpenter's house. Before they built a walk-in freezer on top of it, the trapdoor led down to the carpenter's cellar."

"Where the coffins are," Mosaic said.

"Yes," I said. "Exactly. But one of you knew about that, and when you all decided to come back to find out what happened to Justin, that person knew to look underneath the hotel, because they'd been there before."

"What are you saying?" Georgina asked. "Are you accusing one of us of killing Justin?"

"She didn't say that," Hogan said.

"No?" Georgina rounded on Hogan, and said, "She just implied that one of us knew there was a trapdoor down there, and that they went looking for Justin. She's implying that the same person must have been there before."

"And when Niinu told Justin how he could sneak back into the hotel," I said.

"Somebody followed him and locked the trapdoor," Simonsen said in rusty but passable

English, as he took a step away from the wall. "Which makes it murder."

"You can't prove that," Georgina said. She turned to the others. "They can't prove it."

Everyone else stayed quiet, choosing to look at their feet, or at the walls, but not at each, and not at Simonsen or me. All apart from Claudia. She looked straight at me, and, as I opened my mouth to speak, she nodded with what felt like reluctant encouragement.

"Of everyone in the group, you miss him the most," I said, looking at Claudia. "Don't you?"

She nodded.

"You knew about the cellar."

Another nod.

"And you know how to use a power screwdriver."

"It's not difficult," Hogan said. Jordan shushed him.

"So, when you came back," I said. "You went down to the cellar, just as soon as you'd checked in."

"Yes," she said.

"Because that was the last place you had seen Justin."

"Yes."

"Claudia?" Jordan said. "You locked Justin inside the freezer?"

Claudia shrank on her chair, slumping against the backrest as the energy drained out of her, along with her confession. She had yet to admit to anything, but that didn't stop the others from speculating, accusing, and assuming the moral high ground. I felt it was time to bring them all down to the same level, for Claudia's sake, for Justin's and for Niinu's. I looked over to the table where Niinu sat by the window. Niinu reached under the table and pulled out a cardboard box full of Justin's envelopes. Bradley was the first to see it, and he stiffened in his seat. One by one, the others stopped talking.

"You asked me to investigate," I said, taking the box from Niinu. "But I think what you really wanted, was help in finding these."

"And what are they?" Hogan asked.

"Insurance."

"What?"

"These are Justin's copies of all the policies he ever wrote. The ones Bradley was looking for when he cleared out Justin's office."

"I thought you got everything," Georgina whispered.

"No, *George*," Bradley said. "You know I didn't. Why the hell else would we come back here?"

"These letters," I said, "link all of you to Justin. The policies show how each of you used each other to make you and Justin some money. He brought you together, not as friends, but to use you. And then, when he said he was coming to Greenland, that he'd met someone, you didn't like the idea, did you?"

"You're just guessing," Mosaic said.

"Am I? Why would Jordan sit by the door in the reception when Justin went out for a walk? Why would none of you leave him alone, and if he was with one person, you quickly made sure *they* weren't alone. Jordan," I said, turning to look at her. "You said Justin could anticipate disaster."

"Yes?"

"Well, he did. He anticipated this. So, he prepared for it. He sent copies of everything to the hotel, leaving them with Niinu."

"He sent everything here?" Hogan said.

"Yes."

"And all the letters are in that box?"

"All but one," I said.

Niinu stood up and pulled the last envelope from her back pocket. She wiped at the tears on her cheeks, and then took a long breath, holding it as she opened the crumpled envelope. "This was his last letter," she said. Her voice grew stronger as she read, and the pain in her eyes turned into anger, as she stared at the people she thought were Justin's friends. "*…I've done bad things, Niinu, but I'm going to make it right. I'll start again. When I come back to Greenland, it will be for the last time.*" Niinu folded the letter back into the envelope. She pressed it to her chest, and said, "He promised he wouldn't leave, and he didn't. He's still here. He'll never leave."

I waited for Niinu to sit down, and then took a step towards the nearest table. I put down the box, pausing for a second, wondering what I would say next, wondering how to follow Niinu's reading of Justin's last promise – his promise to her.

I was moved, and I took another moment to hold back a tear, dropping my guard for a moment, just long enough for Georgina to push off her seat and make a grab for the box.

She almost made it to the door, only to stop as Iinta met her halfway, peeling back his fist, before slamming it into her nose. Georgina crumpled to the ground, tossing the box above her head, and spilling Justin's envelopes like disembodied wings into the air.

Hogan was the first to reach for the nearest envelope, tearing the paper out of it, quickly followed by Mosaic, Jordan and Bradley. Only Claudia remained seated, resigned to her fate, just a breath away from confessing.

"For God's sake, Iinta," Simonsen said, as he strode across the room towards him. "You promised."

I smiled as Iinta shrugged, accepting the cuffs that Simonsen slapped around his wrists before returning to his seat with a smug, and, in my opinion, thoroughly deserved grin on his face.

Bradley was the first to look up, and the only one to actually look at the papers. The others were too busy tearing them into small pieces.

"These are menus," he said. "Photocopies."

"Yes," I said, as the others slowly realised what was happening. "You could say Justin anticipated this."

"And the real ones?" Bradley asked, as he stood up.

"Are in a safe place," Simonsen said.

I helped Georgina to her feet and into a chair, plucking a serviette from the table to soak up the blood streaming from her nose.

"Constable," Jordan said, as she found a seat.

"Yes?"

"Do you remember what I asked you, during the interview?"

"You wanted to know if we could arrest you, for crimes committed in America."

"That's right," Jordan said. "And you told me that as long as no crimes had been committed in Greenland…"

"Then you were okay," I said.

"Okay. Thank you, honey. I just wanted to be sure."

"I understand," I said. "But there is just one thing." I felt the curl of my lips before I started to speak, but there was nothing I could do to stop the smile from infecting my voice, when I said, "One of you – maybe more than one – locked me in the freezer. That's a crime, if you didn't know. Attempted murder, no less. And it was committed in Greenland." I pointed at the empty cardboard box and the fake letters strewn across the dining room. "Of course, we're going to have to read all these letters – the real ones – if we're going to find out the motive for such a crime. And I think, Chief," I said, looking at Simonsen, "we might need some help with that."

"My English really isn't that good," he said. "I think we'll need some outside help. But until then. The beaches are closed, no one gets on or off the island."

I frowned as Simonsen started to laugh.

"*Jaws*," he said, before ordering everyone to sit down so he and Danielsen could start to process them.

I turned my back on the confusion and walked over to Niinu's table. I found an extra chair and sat down beside her and Juuliu.

"It's not going to be easy," I said. "And there will be lots of questions. But the Chief promised to look after you."

Niinu took my hand and nodded. "*Qujanaq*. Thank you."

"Don't mention it," I said.

I peeled off Niinu's fleece and hung it on the back of the chair, said goodnight, and then walked to the dining room door. Iinta caught my eye and grinned as I passed him.

"Behave," I said, as I walked out of the dining room, leaving Simonsen and Danielsen with the Americans. I had found my third missing person, and I was done for the night.

Epilogue

"It was Claudia," Simonsen said, as he drove Iinta and I to the heliport the next morning. "She put the tongs in the kitchen door. She confessed right after you went to bed. She confessed to everything."

"Just Claudia?"

"No," he said. "She said Georgina made her do it." Simonsen slowed as a gaggle of lively puppies tumbled across the road. "It seems Georgina was a bit of a ring leader. Once Claudia confessed, they all did. All of them pointing fingers at her."

"Which is strange," I said, thinking that it was Bradley who had the most to lose.

"Until you remember the dogs," Simonsen said, beeping the patrol car's horn at the last of the puppies as it flopped down in front of us. "She's a veterinarian who wants to breed her own dogs. They'll never let her do that if they think she intentionally had dogs killed to make a profit."

"It was Jordan who insured Georgina's dogs."

"And Claudia who killed them."

Iinta snorted and I turned to see him shake his head.

"Exactly," Simonsen said, tilting the rear-view mirror so he could look at Iinta.

"Well," I said, as Simonsen parked outside the heliport. "I hope I never get stranded here again."

"Agreed."

Simonsen tapped two cigarettes out of a packet, and nodded for Iinta to join him for a smoke before the helicopter left for the mainland. I took a moment to look at the heart-shaped mountain that gave Uummannaq its name, wondering when or if I would return.

Iinta was far less chatty than Tikaajaat, sipping his coffee as we flew over Disko Bay with little more than a grunt and a shrug of his shoulders by way of conversation. I settled into my seat, content to stare out of the window, as I thought about Niinu and Juuliu, and the promise Simonsen had made to help them. Growing up in Nuuk, though small in comparison to the big cities of Denmark, and even bigger ones further afield, it was easy to forget how intimate life was in the smaller villages and settlements of Greenland. It made police work both varied and interesting, though not without its fair share of tragedy. This time, it was a visitor who had died, but all too often it was a member of the community, someone who would be missed by everyone who knew them, in varying degrees.

I must have been more affected by Justin's disappearance than I thought, as I found myself unusually sympathetic when I thought of Sergeant Duneq, no doubt waiting to berate me back in Nuuk, when he discovered that I had been locked in a freezer, that I had conducted an unofficial *international* investigation, which developed into a murder inquiry, or manslaughter at the very least. It was all in Simonsen's report, and, as my supervisor,

Duneq would have made it his priority to read it. I could just picture his jowls wobbling in anticipation of the tongue-lashing he would give me – as public as possible – the minute I arrived back at the station. But, in my most sympathetic moment, I was ready to thank Duneq for assigning me to prisoner escort, with the added thought that he did have a plan, and that he was working on my transition from newly trained police recruit straight out of the academy, to a competent constable, capable of pulling her weight no matter the assignment.

I held onto that thought as we landed in Ilulissat, the wheels bumping on the newly thawed runway as the month of May warmed up in anticipation of the short spring before summer.

It was Iinta who brought me back to earth, challenging my thoughts about Sergeant Duneq, when he plucked the in-flight magazine from the rack in the airport waiting lounge, and opened it to the article about me and the Greenland Missing Persons desk.

As soon as I saw the headline, followed by the photo, I understood that even if Duneq had a grand plan to expose me to the varied life of a police officer in Greenland, he would not be able to restrain himself once he read the article. I pulled out my smartphone as Iinta read the article, opened my calendar and deleted all the private dates and arrangements I had made for the weekends in the foreseeable future. I had no doubt I would be working the Friday through Sunday evening shifts long into the summer.

"What do you think?" I asked, when Iinta was

finished with the article.

"Who is Sergeant Duneq?" he asked, tapping a dirty nail beside Duneq's name in the article.

"My boss."

"Hmm," he said.

"What does *hmm* mean?"

Iinta said nothing more. He didn't have to. We both knew I was in trouble.

The End

About the Author

Christoffer Petersen is the author's pen name. He lives in Denmark. Chris started writing stories about Greenland while teaching in Qaanaaq, the largest village in the very north of Greenland – the population peaked at 600 during the two years he lived there. Chris spent a total of seven years in Greenland, teaching in remote communities and at the Police Academy in the capital of Nuuk.

Chris continues to be inspired by the vast icy wilderness of the Arctic and his books have a common setting in the region, with a Scandinavian influence. He has also watched enough Bourne movies to no longer be surprised by the plot, but not enough to get bored.

You can find Chris in Denmark or online here:

www.christoffer-petersen.com

By the Same Author

THE GREENLAND CRIME SERIES
featuring Constable David Maratse
SEVEN GRAVES, ONE WINTER Book 1
BLOOD FLOE Book 2
WE SHALL BE MONSTERS Book 3
INSIDE THE BEAR'S CAGE Book 4
WHALE HEART Book 5

Short Stories from the same series

KATABATIC
CONTAINER
TUPILAQ
THE LAST FLIGHT
THE HEART THAT WAS A WILD GARDEN
QIVITTOQ
THE THUNDER SPIRITS
ILULIAQ
SCRIMSHAW
ASIAQ
CAMP CENTURY
INUK
DARK CHRISTMAS
POISON BERRY
NORTHERN MAIL
SIKU

VIRUSI
THE WOMEN'S KNIFE
ICE, WIND & FIRE

THE GREENLAND TRILOGY
featuring Konstabel Fenna Brongaard
THE ICE STAR Book 1
IN THE SHADOW OF THE MOUNTAIN Book 2
THE SHAMAN'S HOUSE Book 3

MADE IN DENMARK
Short Stories featuring Milla Moth set in Denmark
DANISH DESIGN Story 1

THE POLARPOL ACTION THRILLERS
*featuring Sergeant Petra "Piitalaat" Jensen,
Etienne Gagnon, Hákon Sigurðsson & more*
NORTHERN LIGHT Book 1
MOUNTAIN GHOST Book 2

THE DETECTIVE FREJA HANSEN SERIES
set in Denmark and Scotland
FELL RUNNER Introductory novella
BLACKOUT INGÉNUE

THE WOLF CRIMES SERIES
set in Denmark, Alaska and Ukraine
PAINT THE DEVIL Book 1
LOST IN THE WOODS Book 2
CHERNOBYL WOLVES Book 3

THE WHEELMAN SHORTS
Short Stories featuring Noah Lee set in Australia

PULP DRIVER Story 1

THE DARK ADVENT SERIES
featuring Police Commissioner
Petra "Piitalaat" Jensen set in Greenland
THE CALENDAR MAN Book 1
THE TWELFTH NIGHT Book 2
INVISIBLE TOUCH Book 3
NORTH STAR BAY Book 4

UNDERCOVER GREENLAND
featuring Eko Simigaq and Inniki Rasmussen
NARKOTIKA Book 1

CAPTAIN ERRONEOUS SMITH
featuring Captain Erroneous Smith
THE ICE CIRCUS Book 1

THE BOLIVIAN GIRL
a hard-hitting military and political thriller series
THE BOLIVIAN GIRL Book 1

GUERRILLA GREENLAND
featuring Constable David Maratse
ARCTIC STATE Novella 1
ARCTIC REBEL Novella 2

GREENLAND MISSING PERSONS novellas
featuring Constable Petra "Piitalaat" Jensen
THE BOY WITH THE NARWHAL TOOTH
THE GIRL WITH THE RAVEN TONGUE
THE SHIVER IN THE ARCTIC
THE FEVER IN THE WATER

CPSIA information can be obtained
at www.ICGtesting.com
Printed in the USA
LVHW090724140821
695316LV00013B/121